SO LOST

(A Faith Bold Mystery —Book Six)

BLAKE PIERCE

Blake Pierce

Blake Pierce is the USA Today bestselling author of the RILEY PAGE mystery series, which includes seventeen books. Blake Pierce is also the author of the MACKENZIE WHITE mystery series, comprising fourteen books; of the AVERY BLACK mystery series, comprising six books; of the KERI LOCKE mystery series, comprising five books; of the MAKING OF RILEY PAIGE mystery series, comprising six books; of the KATE WISE mystery series, comprising seven books; of the CHLOE FINE psychological suspense mystery, comprising six books; of the JESSIE HUNT psychological suspense thriller series, comprising thirty-one books; of the AU PAIR psychological suspense thriller series, comprising three books; of the ZOE PRIME mystery series, comprising six books; of the ADELE SHARP mystery series, comprising sixteen books, of the EUROPEAN VOYAGE cozy mystery series, comprising six books; of the LAURA FROST FBI suspense thriller, comprising eleven books; of the ELLA DARK FBI suspense thriller, comprising sixteen books (and counting); of the A YEAR IN EUROPE cozy mystery series, comprising nine books, of the AVA GOLD mystery series, comprising six books; of the RACHEL GIFT mystery series, comprising ten books (and counting); of the VALERIE LAW mystery series, comprising nine books (and counting); of the PAIGE KING mystery series, comprising eight books (and counting); of the MAY MOORE mystery series, comprising eleven books; of the CORA SHIELDS mystery series, comprising eight books (and counting); of the NICKY LYONS mystery series, comprising eight books (and counting), of the CAMI LARK mystery series, comprising eight books (and counting), of the AMBER YOUNG mystery series, comprising five books (and counting), of the DAISY FORTUNE mystery series, comprising five books (and counting), of the FIONA RED mystery series, comprising eight books (and counting), of the FAITH BOLD mystery series, comprising eight books (and counting), of the JULIETTE HART mystery series, comprising five books (and counting), of the MORGAN CROSS mystery series, comprising five books (and counting), and of the new FINN WRIGHT mystery series, comprising five books (and counting).

An avid reader and lifelong fan of the mystery and thriller genres, Blake loves to hear from you, so please feel free to visit www.blakepierceauthor.com to learn more and stay in touch.

ISBN: 978-1-0943-8263-0

BOOKS BY BLAKE PIERCE

FINN WRIGHT MYSTERY SERIES
WHEN YOU'RE MINE (Book #1)
WHEN YOU'RE SAFE (Book #2)
WHEN YOU'RE CLOSE (Book #3)
WHEN YOU'RE SLEEPING (Book #4)
WHEN YOU'RE SANE (Book #5)

MORGAN CROSS MYSTERY SERIES
FOR YOU (Book #1)
FOR RAGE (Book #2)
FOR LUST (Book #3)
FOR WRATH (Book #4)
FOREVER (Book #5)

JULIETTE HART MYSTERY SERIES
NOTHING TO FEAR (Book #1)
NOTHING THERE (Book #2)
NOTHING WATCHING (Book #3)
NOTHING HIDING (Book #4)
NOTHING LEFT (Book #5)

FAITH BOLD MYSTERY SERIES
SO LONG (Book #1)
SO COLD (Book #2)
SO SCARED (Book #3)
SO NORMAL (Book #4)
SO FAR GONE (Book #5)
SO LOST (Book #6)
SO ALONE (Book #7)
SO FORGOTTEN (Book #8)

FIONA RED MYSTERY SERIES
LET HER GO (Book #1)
LET HER BE (Book #2)
LET HER HOPE (Book #3)

LET HER WISH (Book #4)
LET HER LIVE (Book #5)
LET HER RUN (Book #6)
LET HER HIDE (Book #7)
LET HER BELIEVE (Book #8)

DAISY FORTUNE MYSTERY SERIES
NEED YOU (Book #1)
CLAIM YOU (Book #2)
CRAVE YOU (Book #3)
CHOOSE YOU (Book #4)
CHASE YOU (Book #5)

AMBER YOUNG MYSTERY SERIES
ABSENT PITY (Book #1)
ABSENT REMORSE (Book #2)
ABSENT FEELING (Book #3)
ABSENT MERCY (Book #4)
ABSENT REASON (Book #5)

CAMI LARK MYSTERY SERIES
JUST ME (Book #1)
JUST OUTSIDE (Book #2)
JUST RIGHT (Book #3)
JUST FORGET (Book #4)
JUST ONCE (Book #5)
JUST HIDE (Book #6)
JUST NOW (Book #7)
JUST HOPE (Book #8)

NICKY LYONS MYSTERY SERIES
ALL MINE (Book #1)
ALL HIS (Book #2)
ALL HE SEES (Book #3)
ALL ALONE (Book #4)
ALL FOR ONE (Book #5)
ALL HE TAKES (Book #6)
ALL FOR ME (Book #7)
ALL IN (Book #8)

CORA SHIELDS MYSTERY SERIES
UNDONE (Book #1)
UNWANTED (Book #2)
UNHINGED (Book #3)
UNSAID (Book #4)
UNGLUED (Book #5)
UNSTABLE (Book #6)
UNKNOWN (Book #7)
UNAWARE (Book #8)

MAY MOORE SUSPENSE THRILLER
NEVER RUN (Book #1)
NEVER TELL (Book #2)
NEVER LIVE (Book #3)
NEVER HIDE (Book #4)
NEVER FORGIVE (Book #5)
NEVER AGAIN (Book #6)
NEVER LOOK BACK (Book #7)
NEVER FORGET (Book #8)
NEVER LET GO (Book #9)
NEVER PRETEND (Book #10)
NEVER HESITATE (Book #11)

PAIGE KING MYSTERY SERIES
THE GIRL HE PINED (Book #1)
THE GIRL HE CHOSE (Book #2)
THE GIRL HE TOOK (Book #3)
THE GIRL HE WISHED (Book #4)
THE GIRL HE CROWNED (Book #5)
THE GIRL HE WATCHED (Book #6)
THE GIRL HE WANTED (Book #7)
THE GIRL HE CLAIMED (Book #8)

VALERIE LAW MYSTERY SERIES
NO MERCY (Book #1)
NO PITY (Book #2)
NO FEAR (Book #3)
NO SLEEP (Book #4)
NO QUARTER (Book #5)
NO CHANCE (Book #6)

NO REFUGE (Book #7)
NO GRACE (Book #8)
NO ESCAPE (Book #9)

RACHEL GIFT MYSTERY SERIES
HER LAST WISH (Book #1)
HER LAST CHANCE (Book #2)
HER LAST HOPE (Book #3)
HER LAST FEAR (Book #4)
HER LAST CHOICE (Book #5)
HER LAST BREATH (Book #6)
HER LAST MISTAKE (Book #7)
HER LAST DESIRE (Book #8)
HER LAST REGRET (Book #9)
HER LAST HOUR (Book #10)

AVA GOLD MYSTERY SERIES
CITY OF PREY (Book #1)
CITY OF FEAR (Book #2)
CITY OF BONES (Book #3)
CITY OF GHOSTS (Book #4)
CITY OF DEATH (Book #5)
CITY OF VICE (Book #6)

A YEAR IN EUROPE
A MURDER IN PARIS (Book #1)
DEATH IN FLORENCE (Book #2)
VENGEANCE IN VIENNA (Book #3)
A FATALITY IN SPAIN (Book #4)

ELLA DARK FBI SUSPENSE THRILLER
GIRL, ALONE (Book #1)
GIRL, TAKEN (Book #2)
GIRL, HUNTED (Book #3)
GIRL, SILENCED (Book #4)
GIRL, VANISHED (Book 5)
GIRL ERASED (Book #6)
GIRL, FORSAKEN (Book #7)
GIRL, TRAPPED (Book #8)
GIRL, EXPENDABLE (Book #9)

GIRL, ESCAPED (Book #10)
GIRL, HIS (Book #11)
GIRL, LURED (Book #12)
GIRL, MISSING (Book #13)
GIRL, UNKNOWN (Book #14)
GIRL, DECEIVED (Book #15)
GIRL, FORLORN (Book #16)

LAURA FROST FBI SUSPENSE THRILLER
ALREADY GONE (Book #1)
ALREADY SEEN (Book #2)
ALREADY TRAPPED (Book #3)
ALREADY MISSING (Book #4)
ALREADY DEAD (Book #5)
ALREADY TAKEN (Book #6)
ALREADY CHOSEN (Book #7)
ALREADY LOST (Book #8)
ALREADY HIS (Book #9)
ALREADY LURED (Book #10)
ALREADY COLD (Book #11)

EUROPEAN VOYAGE COZY MYSTERY SERIES
MURDER (AND BAKLAVA) (Book #1)
DEATH (AND APPLE STRUDEL) (Book #2)
CRIME (AND LAGER) (Book #3)
MISFORTUNE (AND GOUDA) (Book #4)
CALAMITY (AND A DANISH) (Book #5)
MAYHEM (AND HERRING) (Book #6)

ADELE SHARP MYSTERY SERIES
LEFT TO DIE (Book #1)
LEFT TO RUN (Book #2)
LEFT TO HIDE (Book #3)
LEFT TO KILL (Book #4)
LEFT TO MURDER (Book #5)
LEFT TO ENVY (Book #6)
LEFT TO LAPSE (Book #7)
LEFT TO VANISH (Book #8)
LEFT TO HUNT (Book #9)
LEFT TO FEAR (Book #10)

LEFT TO PREY (Book #11)
LEFT TO LURE (Book #12)
LEFT TO CRAVE (Book #13)
LEFT TO LOATHE (Book #14)
LEFT TO HARM (Book #15)
LEFT TO RUIN (Book #16)

THE AU PAIR SERIES
ALMOST GONE (Book#1)
ALMOST LOST (Book #2)
ALMOST DEAD (Book #3)

ZOE PRIME MYSTERY SERIES
FACE OF DEATH (Book#1)
FACE OF MURDER (Book #2)
FACE OF FEAR (Book #3)
FACE OF MADNESS (Book #4)
FACE OF FURY (Book #5)
FACE OF DARKNESS (Book #6)

A JESSIE HUNT PSYCHOLOGICAL SUSPENSE SERIES
THE PERFECT WIFE (Book #1)
THE PERFECT BLOCK (Book #2)
THE PERFECT HOUSE (Book #3)
THE PERFECT SMILE (Book #4)
THE PERFECT LIE (Book #5)
THE PERFECT LOOK (Book #6)
THE PERFECT AFFAIR (Book #7)
THE PERFECT ALIBI (Book #8)
THE PERFECT NEIGHBOR (Book #9)
THE PERFECT DISGUISE (Book #10)
THE PERFECT SECRET (Book #11)
THE PERFECT FAÇADE (Book #12)
THE PERFECT IMPRESSION (Book #13)
THE PERFECT DECEIT (Book #14)
THE PERFECT MISTRESS (Book #15)
THE PERFECT IMAGE (Book #16)
THE PERFECT VEIL (Book #17)
THE PERFECT INDISCRETION (Book #18)
THE PERFECT RUMOR (Book #19)

KERI LOCKE MYSTERY SERIES

A TRACE OF DEATH (Book #1)

A TRACE OF MURDER (Book #2)

A TRACE OF VICE (Book #3)

A TRACE OF CRIME (Book #4)

A TRACE OF HOPE (Book #5)

PROLOGUE

Marvin woke with a gasp and tried to sit, but his head smacked on something hard and he collapsed back with a cry, ears ringing. He tried to lift his hand to his head, but it smacked against the same hard substance.

He took a deep breath and tried to calm his pounding heart. Where was he? The air smelled stale and musty, a moldy smell that reminded him of his grandfather's old compost pile. He and Grandpa used to dig for earthworms to use when they went fishing at the old creek behind their house.

Well, he wasn't in a compost pile, so where was he? And what was this wooden box he was—

Oh God.

Oh no.

Oh God, *no!*

"Help!" he screamed. "Help me!"

He tried to pound on the lid of what he now realized was a coffin, but the coffin was narrow, and he couldn't get any force behind the blows. The sound echoed inside the confines of the box, but he knew no one could hear him outside.

Outside. Outside was six feet of solid earth. He had been buried alive.

Panic surged again, but he forced himself to stay calm. He knew that panic would only hasten his death. He tried to think about how he had gotten here. If he could remember what happened last night, maybe he could figure out how he had made it here and—

And what? Call the police? He patted his pocket and wasn't particularly surprised to find it empty. No cell phone. No way to call for help.

Not that it mattered. He couldn't remember anything after the bar. He had arrived after work to have a few drinks before going home and enjoying a mandatory off day before once more being on call all day. The day had been hard. They had had to perform CPR on a toddler who had climbed through the doggy door to his backyard and fallen into the pool. The kid still wasn't breathing on his own when they reached the hospital, and he didn't need to be a doctor to know that if he wasn't breathing on his own after that long, he wasn't breathing on his own ever again.

So, he was going to enjoy a few drinks, just enough to numb the pain so he could survive another day in hell. He was well on his way through his second Long Island iced tea when he felt a hand on his shoulder.

And then he was here. And it didn't matter if that girl was real or if she had something to do with this because it was too late. He was going to die. He was going to die, and there was nothing he could do about it.

A tinny scratch like the static from an old radio cut through his panic. He jumped and cried out, hitting his head again. It started to throb, a dull ache behind his temples, and he didn't know if the ache was due to hitting his head twice or to the thinning oxygen. Already he felt like he couldn't catch his breath. He didn't have long.

Good evening, a robotic voice carried through the coffin. It sounded exactly like an old radio host, and he realized that there must be a radio inside the coffin. Marvin's heart leapt with hope.

"Yes, hello?" he cried. "Can you help me? I'm stuck inside one of the graves. I—I don't know where I am, but I think it's one of the freshly dug graves. I mean, it has to be, I would only have been here a few minutes or I would already have…" He squeezed back tears.

Before he could speak again, the voice continued. *By now you've figured out that you're in a coffin. The time is now midnight. You have perhaps four or five hours of air left before you asphyxiate to death.*

"Yes, I know!" he cried out. "Can you help…" His voice trailed off as he realized the horrible truth. "Oh my God. You're the guy. You're the guy trying to kill me."

Hot tears leaked from the corners of his eyes. His heart pounded and his head ached. The voice continued, calm and cultured. *There's still hope. There's a string somewhere in the coffin. That string is connected to a bell at the surface of the grave. If you sound the bell, there's a chance the night watchman will hear it and know that you've been buried alive.*

He began searching frantically for the string, banging his hands all over the box and all over himself, twisting to see if maybe he was lying on the string, in his panic not thinking that the string would have to be hanging down from the top of the coffin.

Be calm, the voice reminded him. *Don't panic. The more you panic, the more you use your available oxygen and the less time you have to summon rescue. Keep in control and look for the string. It's your* only *chance.*

"Please," he sobbed. "Please let me go. I'll do anything you ask me to. I'll do anything, just please don't kill me."

Look carefully, the voice replied impassively. *Time moves quickly in the dark.*

"Fuck you!" he shouted. "Why are you doing this?"

There was no response. "Dammit!" he shouted, pounding his hand against the top of the coffin again.

He sobbed once more, and the pounding in his head increased. He forced himself to remain calm and resumed his search for the string. The seconds seemed to tick by with aching slowness, but for all he knew, they were moving at breakneck speed, each one that passed lessening the amount of time he had to save his own life.

He had to move quickly. He had to—

There it was! There was the string!

Marvin cried out with hope. "Okay," he whispered to himself. "Okay, okay, you're okay. You'll be okay."

He thought of his young daughter at home with his wife. Just that morning, she had read her favorite book to him all by herself. He had grinned so widely. He had hugged her so tightly. He was so proud of her. His wife made him promise to be safe and come home soon.

If he had only skipped the bar and just gone straight home, he would be in bed with his wife right now, staying up and watching their little girl through the monitor they still kept in her room even though she would be starting kindergarten next year.

He would be okay. He would come home to them. He had to.

He tugged the string. There was no sound. He nearly panicked again until he reminded himself that he wouldn't be able to hear the bell under six feet of earth, but that didn't mean there wasn't one. He tugged hard, pulling until he felt the string tighten and then continuing to pull, over and over and over.

There was another tinny scratch, and he released a choked laugh of desperate hope. "Hello?" he called. "Can you hear me? I'm in a grave. I'm… do you hear the bell? I was buried alive, can you help—"

Good evening. By now you've figured out that you're in a coffin. The time is now midnight. You have perhaps four or five hours of air left before you asphyxiate to death. There's still hope.

He listened to the voice repeat the message, and dread slowly filled his trembling limbs.

murdered as a teenager—until they died of starvation or heart failure. The name Wax Murderer came about when some clever reporter decided the idea of living statues reminded him of that old horror movie about people encased in wax and placed in a museum.

She had come home from that case ready to make a new start with David. She was prepared to acknowledge that she had been emotionally unavailable and afraid of commitment and tell him that she was ready to let go of the past and work toward a future with him.

She had met him for dinner to tell him all of this only for him to say that he wanted to take a break. He wasn't sure anymore if there was a future for them, and he didn't know if he wanted to wait to find out and risk having his heart broken.

She hadn't heard from him since then. At his request, she hadn't contacted him, and the silence weighed heavily on her with each passing day. Her birthday was next month, and she was terrified that the day would pass without a text from him.

She realized now that she had been holding out hope that he would reach out to her and that this would all be over. She thought that he was only angry and that when he got over it, he would call her, they would make up, and everything would be hunky-dory again.

Now she worried that she had misread the situation and that he never intended to take her back. If her birthday came and went with no contact, then there would be no doubt.

She reached for the next file and her fingers fell on an empty desk. She had finished her paperwork.

She looked at Turk, who sat patiently next to the desk, watching the TV through the break room window. "Looks like we're off early today, Turk. What do you think we should do? Pizza and sitcoms?"

The dog met Faith's eyes, then looked pointedly at her phone.

She blushed a little and said, "Yeah, you're right. You never know until you try."

She reached for her phone and started typing, but she didn't know what to say. She tried *Hey, David! It's me!*

She shook her head and erased *It's me!*

Hey, do you want to have dinner tonight?

No, too direct.

Thinking about you and was wondering if you wanted to see me.

Too desperate.

She thought about just sending *Hey, David!* and waiting for him to respond.

What if he didn't, though? Should she follow up later and ask him to dinner? Maybe she should forget about dinner and just ask him for coffee the next day. That was much lower pressure than dinner. And the first time they had gone out, it was to a coffee shop. Well, actually, their first *date* date was dinner. They just ran into each other at the coffee shop, or rather Turk led her there to meet him.

Poor Turk. He missed his vet just like Faith missed her boyfriend.

That was it! She could make an appointment for Turk! Then he'd *have* to see her.

Hey, I was wondering if I could bring Turk in tomorrow for his physical? It's been six months, and he still has a bit of a limp when he wakes up in the morning. Can you check it out, and...

She read the text and sighed in frustration. Now she looked desperate and a little bit crazy. Really? Trying to force him to see her by making up a problem with Turk that he would immediately see wasn't there? Was she *that* desperate?

She was. There was no hiding it. She absolutely was that desperate, and there was no way she could text him without that becoming clear.

This was stupid. She wasn't going to satisfy her concerns by texting him, and she wasn't doing herself any favors by holding onto hope that might be false. She would go see him. She checked her phone. Four-thirty. If she hurried, she could catch David at his office. If he told her to piss off, then she would know.

But maybe he wouldn't. Maybe he would at least listen to her.

She got up from her desk and dropped the paperwork off at Clark's office. He was on the phone, but he looked up when she arrived.

"Hey, Faith, you have a second?"

"Oh," she said, "actually, I was just on my way to—"

"This will only take a moment," he said. "It's important."

She sighed inwardly and took a seat in front of his desk. Supervisory Special Agent Gordon Clark was her immediate supervisor. The Boss had assigned him to babysit her after her obsession with the Copycat Donkey Killer case—which everyone simply called the Copycat Killer case—had caused her performance and her professionalism to deteriorate to unacceptable levels. She was out of the hotseat now, but the Boss apparently believed that was due to Clark's leadership and allowed him to stay on as SSA of any cases involving serial or spree killers.

"Hey, I'm gonna call you back," Clark said when Faith sat. He hung up the phone and smiled at her. "How you doin'?"

"I'm good, Gordon," she said, keeping her irritation out of her voice. "I'm in kind of a hurry though, so—"

"Say no more," Clark said, lifting his hand. "I'll make this quick. I've talked with the Boss, and we both think you're ready to help with the Copycat Killer case."

A thrill of excitement and a chill of fear surged through Faith simultaneously. This Copycat Killer was using the same MO as Jethro Trammell, the Donkey Killer who had killed Turk's previous handler and tortured Faith nearly to death herself. Trammell had been shot dead by Michael just before he killed Faith, but this copycat was tying people up and cutting them just like Trammell had. Faith had ignored repeated warnings to let the case go and pursued him for over a year.

Then she stopped. With the help of her therapist, Dr. Franklin West, she had finally managed to overcome that obsession and move on.

And now that she had stopped investigating without permission, Clark was about to give her permission.

"Help how?" she asked.

"A purely consultative basis," he said. "No fieldwork, strict orders. The Boss doesn't want you knocking doors down or interrogating people again, and I agree with him. However, I think you have a keen intellect and a knack for getting into the heads of killers. You're familiar with the case, and it was your efforts that eventually led to us stopping the original Donkey Killer, so I think your perspective would be useful to Desrouleaux and Chavez."

He pulled a file from his desk drawer and slid it over to Faith. "You've probably seen most of that," he said with a chuckle, "from your earlier snooping. There's a little more there now. There have been two more victims in the past three months. That brings the total to twenty-seven."

Faith stared at the file without touching it. Her mind was reeling. "Do Desrouleaux and Chavez know I'm being asked to look at this?"

"They were the ones who asked me," Clark said. "Well, Desrouleaux was. Chavez doesn't know you. That reminds me, you should take her out to lunch sometime. She's a good kid. She'd benefit from some advice from a seasoned veteran like yourself."

"I'll hit her up some time," Faith said, her eyes still planted on the file.

She wasn't sure if she wanted this anymore. On one hand, this was the case that had consumed her thoughts for months. On the other hand, her obsession had brought her nothing but pain or loss, chief of which was the loss that she had just been on her way to regain.

Then again, she wasn't having nightmares anymore. She wasn't moody or anxious anymore. Maybe she was ready.

Or maybe the reason her mind was healing was the fact that she *wasn't* involved with the case.

"Hey, Faith," Clark said gently. "Look, I'll understand if you're not up for this. I won't be offended if you pass. I know this case caused you a lot of grief. I only wanted to give you first right of refusal since the case is so important to you. And I do think you're ready, but if you don't think that, just let me know, and I'll ask someone else to take a look at it."

"No," she said, speaking almost before her mind caught up to her decision. "It's all right. I'll take it."

His eyes brightened, and he smiled. "Wonderful," he said. "Thank you, Faith. I appreciate the help."

"No problem," Faith said, forcing a return smile. "I'll look it over and get back to you with my thoughts."

He gave her a thumbs-up. "You're the best, Faith."

She stood and reached for the file. She half-expected a jolt of electricity to run through her when she touched it, but it felt the same as any other file. She smiled again at Clark, then left the office.

***

"Faith," David said, frozen in shock. "What are you doing here?"

Faith didn't answer right away, not because she didn't have an answer but because she'd forgotten just how attractive David was. His light brown hair fell in soft waves nearly to his shoulders and his bright blue eyes shone like diamonds behind his glasses. His body looked like it belonged on a billboard, and his lips were full and soft, but still rugged and manly and—

She took a deep breath and smiled at him. "I came here to talk to you."

"Oh," he said. "I, uh, I wish you had called first."

"Would you have answered if I did?"

He lowered his eyes and didn't reply for a moment. Finally, he smiled and said, "It's good to see you."

He opened his arms and Faith embraced him. His smile stopped before reaching his eyes and his shoulders were tense under Faith's

It just infuriated him! Where did they get off meddling like that? They were nothing compared to him! Nothing compared to *her*! This was supposed to be his opus! He—the master criminal—versus Faith Bold—the amazing detective! Good versus evil. Right versus wrong. Order versus chaos. It was *perfect*, dammit!

And now? Now it was just another murder case. He was just another perp, and she was just another gumshoe doing her job. If she found him, it wouldn't be the expert detective stopping the master criminal. It would be "an FBI investigation led to the capture of." If he caught her and finished the job Trammell couldn't, then it would be "an agent lost in the line of duty," not "famous FBI detective found dead."

The distinction might seem subtle, but it was an *important* difference!

He lifted his hand and let it fall lightly on the steering wheel. "Goddammit."

Well, he didn't have a choice now. He couldn't kill David. Even if he were willing to risk the heightened chance of discovery, there was no *fun* in killing him now.

He would just have to be patient. He would have to wait and see.

Well, that wasn't entirely true. He couldn't attack her directly, but he could chip away at her defenses subtly, as he had been for the past several months. It was tedious work and not nearly so fulfilling as the other avenues he intended to pursue, but he supposed it would do until he could think of another way to escalate the game.

He pulled into his garage and checked his phone, a habit he'd had since before he knew of his calling. There was only one message, a nagging text from his soon-to-be ex-wife about some procedural thing related to the divorce.

An idea struck him. Perhaps he could get to Faith through that avenue. It was very roundabout, far more so even than the weekly meetings, but it could work. After all, Faith was complex, but those close to her were far more simple. If he could pull the right strings, he could cause one of her pillars to collapse. It wasn't the same as killing her boyfriend, but in many ways, this pillar was a far more important and valuable one than the vet.

Yes. That could work. He would still win.

He just had to play with a little more finesse.

CHAPTER THREE

Michael laughed and kissed the tip of Ellie's nose. Her face wrinkled adorably, and he laughed and kissed her again.

"Stop!" she cried with a giggle, pulling her head back and trying to wiggle out from underneath him.

He kissed her nose again, then again, and she squealed and rolled over, pushing him off. He fell over, laughing again while she scrambled out of bed, red-faced but smiling.

"Why do you like doing that so much?"

"I love the way your face scrunches up," he said. "It's cute."

"But your mustache tickles me when you kiss my nose!" she protested.

"Is that why you never kiss me anymore?" Michael asked, rolling to a sitting position on the edge of the bed.

"Anymore?" she teased. "When did I ever kiss you?"

"Hmm," he said, cocking his head. "That's right. Come to think of it, you haven't given me a good kiss in a while."

He stood and approached Ellie, who giggled and extended a hand to defend herself as she backed up. "Don't you dare!" she cried, grinning playfully.

"Dare what?" Michael asked innocently. "I'm not doing anything."

Ellie continued to back up, circling around the bed to keep the mattress in between them. "Michael!" she warned. "I swear to God, if you tickle me, I'll—Michael!"

He lunged across the bed and swiped at her. She twisted her hips and narrowly avoided his grab, but as she sprinted to the door, squealing and laughing, he caught her around the waist and pulled her down onto the mattress, where he proceeded to tickle her feverishly.

"Michael!" she cried, twisting and writhing underneath him. "Michael, stop!"

She gasped with laughter, tears falling down her face, and Michael said, "Not until you kiss me."

"Never!" she giggled.

"Kiss me," he said. "Kiss me, or I won't stop."

"Oh my God! All right, fine!"

And apparently, it had left a sour taste in Ellie's mouth that still remained.

"At least you met her," Michael insisted lamely, too frustrated to give up the argument even staring down at the hole he was digging himself.

"And at least I'm not *sleeping* with Frank," Ellie shot back.

Michael stared in stunned silence for a moment. When he did speak, all he could manage was an incredulous, "What?"

"I'm saying that *I* don't travel around the country with Frank sleeping in the same hotel room," Ellie said. "You know, the way you and Faith sleep together."

Michael blinked, staggered at the turn this conversation had taken. "Ellie, we don't sleep *together*. We… yes, we sleep in the same room, but that's because the Bureau only pays for one room. We're not having…" He couldn't finish the thought.

"No, but you want to," Ellie fired back.

"No I don't!" Michael shouted. Now he really *was* angry. "Why the hell would I be doing anything with you if I was in love with Faith?"

"I didn't say you were in love," Ellie retorted.

"Don't do that," Michael countered. "Don't try to twist my words. I'm not sleeping with Faith."

"Well, she wants to sleep with you," Ellie replied.

Michael chuckled and shook his head. Ten minutes ago, they were in the middle of very satisfying and very intense sex and now they were arguing over this? "Ellie," he said, trying to be calm, "she's not in love with me. She has a boyfriend."

"And you have a girlfriend. But she still looked at me like she can't wait for me to disappear and stop stealing her Prince away from her."

"Ellie, you're being ridiculous," Michael said.

Once again, he immediately regretted his word choice. Ellie's jaw tightened and she turned and stalked from the room without another word.

Michael sighed and fell back on the bed. He stared upward, his eyes idly following the hills and valleys of the popcorn ceiling as he let the past five minutes soak in.

Faith and Michael had dated for a little over a year, but their relationship had ended over two years ago, shortly before Faith's encounter with the original Donkey Killer left her severely injured. She had been the one to end things between them, and if Michael was being honest, he had been crushed when they broke up. He had believed at the time that he and Faith would marry and spend the rest of their lives together.

But he didn't feel that way anymore. When Faith healed and returned to the Bureau, he thought for a minute that they might pick things up where they left off, but during their first case back together, he noticed a change in Faith. After Trammell, she had grown moody and distant, even cold. She had always been more serious than Michael and had never been particularly affectionate, but she had walls now that Michael couldn't break through.

She was healing now, and the past few months had been much more like the Faith he knew. The anger was receding, and the moodiness and coldness had gone, but the attraction he once felt was gone too. He had found Ellie, and she was the one for him, the only one for him. He viewed Faith more as a sister than a former lover, and the thought of them being romantically involved was absurd.

But he realized now that it didn't look that way to Ellie. She saw the two of them laughing and talking like old friends, saw the mistrust in Faith's eyes and the hostility in Turk's behavior, then had to watch him leave with her for days at a time to solve high-stress cases during the day and take turns showering in the same bathroom at night.

He would never in a million years cheat on Ellie, but he couldn't be upset with her for fearing that.

And, he acknowledged reluctantly, he would have to let go of his irritation over the divorce. Absurd though Ellie's fears might be, from her perspective it was no less absurd than his impatience.

He sighed and rolled out of bed, dressing more slowly and reluctantly than Ellie had. He would have to apologize to her and then do something nice to make up for his behavior. Maybe he would buy her ice cream. Yeah, that's what he would do. He would pick up a pint of that brand she liked, the one with the two guys on the logo, and a card with a picture of a puppy on it.

No, not a puppy. A kitten. That was better. He would get her ice cream and a card, and he would apologize. She would sigh and hug him and tell him she forgave him and then they would snuggle on the couch and watch some sappy romcom before making slow, romantic love and falling asleep in each other's arms.

Everything would be okay by the morning.

He pulled on his boxers and T-shirt and headed for the door.

And his phone rang.

Michael took a deep breath and released it in a heavy sigh. He glanced out the window at the sky, where the twilight was well on its way to darkness.

Only one reason why someone would be calling him this late at night.

He answered his phone without even bothering to look at the number.

"Hey, asshole," Faith's voice came over the phone. "I hope you got your bag packed, because your plane leaves in ten minutes."

Her cheerfulness sounded fake, and Michael guessed she was as unhappy with the late-night interruption as he was. "Hey," he said flatly. "This the call-up?"

"Yep," she said, "you're going to the show, kid."

He sighed again. "Lovely. Am I meeting you at the airport or the office?"

"The office. I guess the Boss likes me again. He's briefing us on the case."

Michael nodded. "All right. I'll be there in twenty."

"Sounds good. Turk and I will meet you there. Tell Ellie I'm sorry."

Not a chance, he thought. "Will do."

He hung up and finished dressing. He stopped and regarded himself in the mirror. He would be thirty-nine years old next week. The uniform he wore was the same one he received fifteen years ago. The physique underneath the uniform was fit and trim—maybe not quite so much as it was when he was twenty-four, but close enough.

The face wasn't bad either. No one would guess him to be in his mid-twenties, but most would probably be at least decently surprised to learn he was only an orbit and a hair away from turning forty. His hair was still dark and full with only a few stray grays at the temples.

His eyes were where the age showed. How did that line go from that old movie? It ain't the years, honey, it's the mileage.

Well, Michael wore his miles in his eyes, which stared back at him with an exhaustion that went far beyond physical. He had seen things that would drive most people insane, and he had seen them at a rate of four or five times per year for over a third of his life. He had spent almost as much time away from home as at home and like many career law enforcement agents, he had never married.

Like many veteran agents, he was trying desperately to change that.

Like many veteran agents, he was failing.

He walked from the bedroom, moving as slowly as a man walking to his execution.

Ellie was in the kitchen making dinner. A stockpot simmered on the stove while she chopped potatoes, her movements as efficient as when she dressed earlier. She didn't look up when he walked into the kitchen and didn't slow her chopping when he leaned over and kissed her cheek.

"I have to go to work," he said softly. "There's a case."

"Okay," Ellie said with false cheerfulness. "I'll see you later."

"I love you," he said.

She didn't respond, continuing to chop away at the potatoes with brisk, businesslike strokes.

Michael waited a moment longer, then turned away and left.

CHAPTER FOUR

"What's up with the long face?"

Michael looked at Faith and replied, "I could ask you the same question."

Faith shrugged. "Boy problems. You?"

"Girl problems."

Michael looked down at Turk, who barked happily and offered the open-mouthed pant that substituted for a smile. Michael chuckled and reached down to ruffle the dog's fur. "At least one of us is happy."

Faith nodded and they started inside. They had recently decided to keep details of their love lives to themselves after conflict over Michael's relationship with Ellie had driven a wedge into their friendship. Besides, Michael was in no mood to talk to anyone about Ellie, and Faith seemed to feel the same about David.

So, Michael and Faith walked inside with grim expressions.

Meanwhile, Turk marched in with clear excitement, wagging his tail and trotting like a puppy three steps ahead of his humans as they entered the building. Michael and Faith received a few polite greetings, but most of the attention was, of course, lavished on the big German shepherd, who had become something of a mascot for the Philadelphia Field Office of the Federal Bureau of Investigation and after playing a key role in a series of high-profile investigations had achieved a level of notoriety among the Bureau as a whole. A month ago, Faith had brought Turk to Quantico for a seminar teaching prospective K9s and their handlers how to detect evidence. Since then, Turk had walked with an air of authority and gravity that Michael found adorable.

But not today. Today, Turk was a puppy again, wagging his tail, barking enthusiastically and rolling over for belly pats, which the agents and analysts present were all too happy to provide.

Michael smiled slightly. He liked the big goofy mutt. He had called in several favors to get Turk assigned to Faith after the Donkey Killer incident, and he was grateful for that. Faith and Turk had developed a close bond and Michael suspected that the dog's solid presence in Faith's life was often the only thing that kept her getting out of bed.

But part of him wished he had kept Turk for himself. He had wanted to get a dog for him and Ellie, but after Turk had inexplicably taken an immediate dislike to Ellie, that plan had gone out the window.

Michael still suspected that Turk's behavior could be explained by jealousy on Faith's side. The two of them might not be romantically involved anymore, but they were still close friends as well as partners, and from day one, Faith had been ambivalent about Ellie. She claimed it was only concern for her friend, but Michael wasn't sure he believed that.

He recalled his argument with Ellie earlier where for the first time she admitted her concern that he and Faith shared hotel rooms on assignment. He didn't believe Faith had any more romantic interest in him than he felt for her, but she might still be possessive of him as though he belonged to her.

Or maybe he was just worked up over the fight with Ellie, and he was overthinking things. God, he hated leaving the house angry.

"Prince! Bold! Turk!" a familiar gruff voice called. "This isn't a damned mixer! Get your asses in my office now! The rest of you back to work!"

The crowd dissipated slowly. A few of the more tenured agents offered exaggerated salutes and acknowledgments to the owner of the voice and earned themselves a glare. Michael, Faith, and Turk proceeded to the office of the Special Agent in Charge of the Philadelphia Field Office, Grant "The Boss" Monroe.

The Boss was a nickname given to Monroe by Jack Preston, a mentor of Michael's and the shining star of the Philadelphia Field Office prior to Faith's ascendance. The Donkey Killer, Jethro Trammell, had killed Preston and nearly killed Turk and Faith during the FBI manhunt that eventually led to Trammell's death at Michael's hands. Preston had been Monroe's favorite back in the day, and he allowed the nickname to stick.

So now, he was known and addressed simply as the Boss or Boss. Gloria Chavez, one of the newest agents, had confided to Michael that she didn't even know his real name, a fact Michael found absolutely hilarious. He'd tried to convince the others not to tell her, but her partner, Desrouleaux, a fifteen-year veteran as no-nonsense as Monroe himself, had spilled the beans and scolded Michael for picking on the new kid.

"Prince!" The Boss's voice cut through his musings. "What did I just say?"

Michael smiled. "I heard you, Boss, but I can't, I'm sorry. I have a girlfriend."

The Boss glared at him. Faith rolled her eyes. Turk made a panting noise that Michael recognized as the dog's way of laughing. He grinned widely into the Boss's glare and the Boss said, "Real funny, Prince. When it's Ellie's body they're digging out of a fresh grave, I'll make sure to laugh too."

Michael's smile vanished. He felt an instinctive twinge of anger at the Boss's words, but he knew he deserved it, so the anger disappeared before it could stick. "Sorry, Boss," he said, "I've had a rough day."

"Suck it up, Prince," the Boss said, and again, Michael had to admit he deserved that. "Marvin Prescott and Barbara Ames had a worse day than you did."

"Those are the victims?" Michael asked.

"Yes," the Boss said, "and consider yourself lucky, because I've only repeated myself to three people in my life and two of them were my parents."

He walked behind the desk and reached into one of the drawers. Faith glanced questioningly at Michael and he shook his head slightly. The message was clear. *I'll talk to you later.*

The Boss tossed a file on the desk and Faith reached over and opened it. Michael whistled when he saw the photographs. "Buried alive, huh?"

"Yep. In graveyards."

"Jesus," Michael said. "This guy's sick."

"They usually are," Faith said.

"The victims were found buried in freshly dug graves in different cemeteries in the Houston area," the Boss explained. "One cemetery was in Houston itself, the other an hour outside of Houston in the town of Humble."

"Any connection between the victims?" Michael asked.

"They're both in the medical field," the Boss replied. "Prescott was a paramedic, Ames was an ICU doctor."

"Did they interact with each other?" Faith asked.

"I don't know," the Boss said. "Ames worked at one of several hospitals contracted with the Houston Fire Department. It's possible that they interacted, but if you want to know for sure, you'll have to dig through their records."

"We'll put it on our list," Faith said.

"They were for sure buried alive?" Michael asked. "Not killed beforehand?"

"Buried alive," the Boss confirmed. "Cause of death asphyxiation. The coroner estimates they were alive around four hours before they ran out of air."

"Christ," Michael whispered. "That's awful."

His mind traveled back to the first case he and Faith had taken after her recovery. A mentally ill man in Morgan County, Missouri, had trapped thirteen women in abandoned wells over seven years. Faith and Michael had been called for the last two of those victims and narrowly saved the life of victim fourteen. Michael could only imagine the terror those women felt as they waited to die.

The killer had been named the Demon of Morgan County because he "dragged his victims to Hell." It was a rather foolish and insensitive nickname, but that tracked with the media.

He wondered what they would call this psycho.

"Interesting thing," the Boss said. "Both graves were rigged with bells so the victims could call for help."

Faith's eyes widened. "Really?"

"Really," the Boss confirmed.

"Were the bells functional?" Michael asked.

"They were functional," the Boss confirmed, "but the victims were buried at night, so there was no one around to hear them."

"Psychological torture," Faith concluded.

"That's the going theory," the Boss confirmed. "Anyway, you two know the drill. Your flight leaves in two hours, so if you need to pack a bag, do it quickly and get to the airport."

The three of them stood. Michael reached for the file, and the Boss pressed his hand on top of it. Faith paused and the Boss said, "He'll meet you outside."

After a moment's hesitation, Faith nodded and led Turk outside.

Michael lifted his eyes to meet Monroe's and the older man said, "You good to work, Prince?"

"Yes," Michael said, a little surprised. "I'm fine. Problems at home, sir. They won't affect my performance on the job."

"They already have," the Boss reminded him. "You're not the kind to daydream. I appreciate all your help getting Bold back up to speed and keeping a lid on her antics until she got her head back in the game, and I hate to sound like I'm picking favorites, but I can't have you losing your shit on me. Bold's not ready to babysit you the way you had to babysit her, so if you need to sit this one out, let me know now and I'll have Clark go with Bold."

"I'm good, Boss," Michael said firmly. "This won't happen again."

The Boss kept his hand pressed on the file a moment longer before nodding and saying, "All right, Prince. Scram."

Michael left the office. Faith and Turk fell into step beside him and headed toward the break room, but Michael passed it without stopping and headed toward the exit.

"No coffee?" Faith asked.

"Not from here," Michael said. "I'll pick up a cup from that Italian place at the airport."

"Wow," Faith said, "you *really* had a bad day."

"Yeah, but I don't want to talk about it," he said grouchily.

"That's fine with me," Faith said. "I don't want to talk about my bad day either."

"Good," Michael replied. "Want to talk about favorite sexual experiences instead?"

Faith rolled her eyes. "No, except to say that none of them involve you."

Michael grinned and did his best Sean Connery impression. "That's not what your mother said."

She chuckled and snorted, and Michael threw his head back and laughed.

"Screw you!" Faith said.

"Well, I would, but apparently, I wasn't any good," Michael quipped.

She rolled her eyes again. "Oh my God. No wonder Ellie's mad at you. Are you like this with her?"

Michael's smile faded, and Faith said, "I'm sorry. Bad joke."

"No, it's all right," Michael said. "It's just a spat. Nothing serious."

"Got it," Faith said. "Well, if it makes you feel better, the 'spat' between me and David seems to be a lot more serious."

He glanced over at her. "Why would that make me feel better?"

"No idea. Forget I said that."

CHAPTER FIVE

Faith looked over at Michael, who kept his gaze stoically ahead at the road but quipped, "Take a picture. It'll add ten pounds, and then I won't look so good, and you won't feel a need to stare."

Faith chuckled and turned away. They had arrived at their hotel just after midnight and, remembering the exhaustion of their last case, they chose to get a good night's sleep and hit the case fresh in the morning.

Michael had suggested they get separate rooms, and when Faith reminded him that the Bureau would only pay for one room, he said he would pay for his. Faith didn't have a good reason to say no, so she didn't protest, but she wondered now if the fight with Ellie had something to do with her. She and Michael had dated before, but their relationship had ended years ago, and Faith saw Michael as more of a brother than a romantic interest. Michael, if anything, was even more enamored with Ellie than she was with David, so there wasn't even the slightest risk of the two of them straying.

But she could see how Ellie might have a problem with Michael sleeping in the same hotel room as his former lover. Those kinds of arrangements were part of the job, but civilians couldn't be expected to understand that.

She wasn't worried. Things would settle. She and Michael had weathered worse storms. As far as Ellie and Michael were concerned… well, she couldn't say much, could she? For all her worries about them, they were still together while she and David weren't.

She pushed the thought away and focused on the case. If they had another Demon on their hands, then they needed to move quickly. Ritualistic killers like these were compulsive. They didn't stop unless they *were* stopped. Two victims in two weeks meant they could expect a third any day.

They reached the graveyard just as the sun crested the horizon. The cemetery was a massive lot spanning possibly forty or fifty acres consisting of manufactured rolling hills with the occasional oak tree sprouting from odd places among the rows. The walking paths were lined with the same white marble that the gravestones were made of. In the center of the cemetery was a massive mausoleum, also of white marble, trimmed with gold and in the same Greek Revivalist style as government buildings.

The whole aesthetic seemed garish to Faith. She never understood why people needed to commercialize death. She was a capitalist through and through, but this was too much. Some things in life should remain sacred.

Their killer clearly didn't feel the same as Faith did. Burying someone alive in a fresh grave was probably the most brutal way Faith could think of to kill someone, psychologically, at least.

They were met at the entrance by a short, heavyset policewoman who looked like a bulldog and was just as thickly muscled. She stuck out a meaty hand, and when Faith took it, she found her grip was as powerful as the rest of her.

"Detective Sergeant Missy St. George," she said in a thick Texas drawl. "I'm the lead on this case. Or I was until you two showed up." She smiled to show there were no hard feelings, and when Turk barked, she looked down at him and said, "I'm sorry. Make that you three."

She removed her bearlike hand from Faith's and held it out for Turk, who lifted his paw and formally placed it in her palm.

She introduced herself to Michael and said, "Wow. You're the pretty boy of the field office, aren't you? You're not looking to date, are you?"

He chuckled politely. "Afraid not."

Missy shrugged. "Oh well. Can't blame a girl for trying."

Her gregarious personality and feminine name contrasted with her wrestler's build, an incongruity that Faith could tell hid a sharp and observant mind. She decided she liked the burly woman.

The burly girly. Faith cracked a smile at that thought.

"All right," Missy said, dropping the smile and adopting a professional expression. "Let's get this road on the show."

She led them to a grave just around the corner behind one of the manufactured hills. It was a good spot to bury someone alive, Faith thought. It was hidden from the road, and since the cemetery was at the top of a high, natural hill, it was a solid three miles between the grave and the rest of civilization. Faith could easily believe that the killer hadn't been noticed.

A moment later, Missy confirmed that thought. "Security didn't hear a damned thing," she said. "According to the owners, this is the first time anyone's ever been harmed on their property. They only had one night watchman, an older guy named Gene. Good guy, but slow-moving and a little hard of hearing."

Faith watched Turk, who sniffed around the grave but didn't seem to find anything of interest. "Have you interviewed the employees?"

"We're in process with that," Missy said. "Nothing's popped up so far."

"Where's the body?" Michael asked.

"Coroner's. Both of them. We haven't received an official report yet, but the COD is pretty clear. They ran out of air."

Michael nodded and gestured to a small bell attached to a length of wire that lay atop the pile of dirt that hours ago had covered the untimely grave of Marvin Prescott. "That the bell?"

"That's it," Missy said, squatting down next to it. "Tiny little guy, isn't it?"

Faith agreed. It wasn't an electronic bell either. Just a small brass bell with a tiny little clapper. It probably sounded like those bells they give mall Santas. Even at night, and even with a security guard with excellent hearing, he would have to be right up close to the bell to know it was being rung.

Their killer definitely intended to torture his victims rather than give them an honest chance.

"So he was messing with them," Michael said, echoing her thoughts.

"That's what we think," Missy replied.

"Any footprints?" Faith replied. "Tire tracks?"

Missy shook her head. "The killer did an excellent job cleaning up after himself. We didn't find anything but signs that he'd covered his tracks."

"No vehicle noise?" Michael asked. "There's no way one person dug a grave and buried a victim in one night."

"Could there be multiple killers?" Faith asked.

"It's possible," Missy said. "It's also possible there's only one killer with an electric vehicle."

"An electric backhoe?" Faith asked.

"Sure," Missy said. "A lot of places are using them now. You don't want to hear diesel engines interrupt your loved one's funeral."

Faith wasn't sure if engine noise was really a concern for a grieving family, but it didn't matter. "Any vehicles found the next morning with low charge? Maybe dirt on them?"

"They're washed weekly, so the fact that one of them might have dirt doesn't mean that it was used. As far as charge goes, their shed's equipped with three hundred fifty kilowatt-hour ultrafast chargers. You could charge something from dead to full in less than an hour."

"Got it," Faith said. "Anything else to note about the scene?"

"Actually, yes," Missy said. "We found a recording device."

Faith's ears perked up. "The killer?"

"Yep. It's at the station. You guys want a ride or do you want to follow me?"

They elected to follow. The station was bustling the way all big city police stations were, but it wasn't unusually hectic. The cemetery was in a nice neighborhood and other than the occasional property crime, there was little business of note.

And, of course, the man who was buried alive.

Missy led them to her desk and offered them coffee, which they accepted. While she went to retrieve the evidence, Faith turned to Michael. "First impressions?"

"Of Missy or the case?"

"The case," she replied, "but nice to know where your mind is."

Michael rolled his eyes and said, "Whatever it is, it's personal or this guy is very crazy. We either have a Demon or we have a revenge killer."

"Why not both?" Faith asked.

Michael shrugged. "That's a possibility too."

Missy returned with a small digital recorder, which she set down on the desk. "Take a listen," she said.

She pressed play and a tinny voice said, "Good evening. By now you've figured out you're in a coffin."

They listened to the message, and when it was over, Missy stopped the recording. "It plays on an endless loop. Doesn't stop until the battery runs out."

"So we know our killer wasn't at the scene for the whole length of time it took them to die," Faith said.

"Most likely not, no."

"We know he's male too," Michael said. "The voice was disguised, but not enough to hide the killer's gender."

"Most likely male, yes."

"And now that I've heard it, I'm leaning toward revenge," Michael replied.

"I don't know," Faith said. "If it was revenge, I feel like the killer would want to see the victim die."

"If he was a crazy, I feel like he would want to stick around for kicks," Michael retorted. "This guy seems too well put-together. It takes a lot of planning to make something like this happen."

"Kenneth Langeveldt wasn't well put-together, and his killings were even more intricate than this," Faith reminded him.

Langeveldt had used a cocktail of powerful narcotics to paralyze people and keep them at his home as stand-ins for his real family, whom he had also murdered. When his victims eventually died of dehydration or heart failure, he would replace them with random people he would stalk and kidnap near his place of business, the Maryland Zoo in Baltimore. He was, as Michael had pointed out, very far from put-together, but had eluded multiple law enforcement agencies before Faith and Michael had stopped him.

"Who found the body?" Faith asked.

"A Ms. Henrietta Eckersley," Missy replied. "Ms., not Miss. She was very particular about that."

"Can we talk to her?" Michael asked.

"Be my guest," Missy said. "I'll let you handle that on your own. I'm drowning in paperwork from another case a few miles away. Kid robbed a convenience store. Owner got spooked and pulled a gun, but his wasn't loaded. The kid's was."

"Oof," Michael said.

"Yep. I guess since you guys are taking lead on the burials, the captain wants me to focus on the convenience store killing. Anyway, I'm available if you need anything, but I'll stay out of your way otherwise. When it's over, I'm treating you all to Texas barbecue, so don't head out without saying goodbye."

"Thanks very much," Michael replied.

They headed to the residence of Ms., not Miss, Henrietta Eckersley. It was a well-manicured Victorian home on a half-acre lot that held a well-manicured garden and a nice but not overly fancy marble fountain. Everything was just so. Faith smiled slightly and imagined a perfectly prim and perfectly proper elderly woman in a well-tailored sundress with silk slippers, a shawl, and a wide sunhat nodding curtly in approval of the landscaping.

Ms. Henrietta Eckersley was exactly that, and wore an almost identical outfit except for the shawl, which was replaced by a surprisingly youthful cardigan that nonetheless seemed only to accentuate the Victorian primness of Ms. Eckersley herself. She greeted the investigators formally and invited them to join her on her porch for sweet tea. Her accent was probably once as thick as Missy's but had softened considerably after years of rich living, a privilege she was not ashamed to admit she gained through marriage.

"My Henry was an austere man, but he was very kind to me." She dabbed very politely at her eyes with a silk handkerchief that probably cost more than Faith's entire outfit. "I miss him so."

"Ms. Eckersley," Michael began.

"Oh please," she replied. "It's Henrietta."

Michael offered her the dazzling movie star smile that women of all ages melted for. Henrietta was no exception, blushing furiously even before Michael replied, "In that case, I'm Michael. Henrietta, can you tell us what you saw yesterday morning?"

"Of course," she replied. "I was visiting my Henry as I always do on Friday mornings, and I noticed that there was a fresh grave nearby. I went over to see if it was someone I knew, but there was no headstone. That struck me as quite odd, so I called management, and when they informed me that there had been no scheduled burials for a week, I immediately called the police. With the blessing of management, of course."

"Did you notice anyone else at the cemetery when you visited?"

"A few," she replied. "Perhaps a dozen. The cemetery is far busier on weekends than on weekdays, of course."

"Anyone seem out of place? Like they didn't belong?"

Henrietta fixed a frank stare on Michael. "Does anyone really belong in a cemetery, Michael?"

We're all heading there one day, Faith thought.

She kept that thought to herself, though, and Michael clarified. "Anyone who seemed suspicious, I mean."

"No, no one suspicious. Not that *I* could tell anyway. My Henry was always a far better judge of human nature than I was, however." She dabbed at her eyes again. "I miss him so."

They asked a few more questions, but Henrietta seemed more interested in talking about her dearly departed husband than about the case, and when she did talk about the case, she had very little to contribute.

They finished their tea and then left, Michael narrowly avoiding a commitment to return for supper.

They stopped for an early lunch at a burger place and over their meal, they discussed the case.

"Whoever the killer is, he must have access to the cemetery at night," Faith said. "Like you pointed out, he would have to have access to heavy equipment to be able to dig that grave in one night."

"Either that, or he had accomplices," Michael suggested.

Faith shook her head. "I doubt it. The more people involved the more tracks to cover, and the greater likelihood they would have missed something. The greater likelihood they would have made noise too and been noticed." She shook her head again. "No, I think we're dealing with a lone wolf."

"So an employee," Michael said.

"Possibly," Faith replied. "Probably."

"We should get a list of the employees scheduled at night," Michael said. "Actually, anyone who could have access."

"Good idea," Faith said, "but we should look at the other gravesite first and see if we might find any more info that could narrow things down."

"Works for me," Michael said. "You want me to drive?"

CHAPTER SIX

Humble was a rapidly growing suburb about thirty minutes outside of Houston but growing rapidly for the wrong reasons. As Houston attempted to gentrify, lower-income families were pushed out to the surrounding communities faster than affordable housing could be built. The homeless problem here wasn't as bad as in cities like San Francisco or Los Angeles, but it was heading that way.

The cemetery, like the town, was several steps down from the pristine marble and manicured lawns of Houston. Faith looked at the dirt paths and patchy brown grass of the Humble Memorial Lawn and decided that there was something to be said about the polish and pomp of the Houston graveyard. This place looked less like a cemetery and more like a dump.

The officer who met them there was a dispassionate, bored-looking man with the unlikely name of Artemis Baxter. The name was the most exciting thing about him. He gave them a rundown of the case in a clipped voice like an auctioneer rattling off the bullet points of an item.

It was essentially the same except this time, it was the morning manager who called the police when he noticed the unmarked and freshly dug grave. Everything else was the same as the first case. There was a bell that was far too small to be heard and a listening device that played the same message as the one in Houston.

When they finished questioning Baxter, Faith asked if he would lead them to the grave. Baxter pointed to his right and said, "Left side, eighth row from the back, fifth plot. You can't miss it. It's the only one without a headstone."

"Got a hot date or something?" Michael said cattily.

Baxter met his eyes. "Double homicide. Nineteen-year-old-kid killed his mother and grandmother. Dad caught him and pulled the gun away before he could use it on himself."

Michael nodded once and averted his eyes. Baxter left without another word and the two special agents exchanged a glance.

"That's the second detective who had to leave us to our own devices to handle a murder committed by a teenager," Faith pointed out. "Something in the water here?"

“It happens all the time when there’s massive inequality,” Michael said. “People feel trapped, and they lash out. It’s not always kids, but it usually is. There’s a reason most street gangsters are under twenty-five.”

“Sheesh,” Faith said. “You’d think they’d do something about that.”

Michael shrugged. “If you say so.”

They reached the grave and once more, Faith watched as Turk sniffed around. The bell and recording device were gone, and there was no police tape cordoning off the scene. The only reason the grave remained open and the dirt untouched was that the cemetery’s owners hadn’t bothered to fill it in yet.

The contrast between these scenes was striking but not relevant to the case. In both places, there were no tracks, and while this cemetery was flat and not at all hidden from the road, Faith had no trouble believing that people in a town like this would see someone digging a grave and push it from their minds.

Not their business.

They started to leave, but Faith stopped when she caught a glance at a nearby headstone. She looked closer and saw the name Carly Ames, born 1937, died 2023. Barbara’s mother or grandmother perhaps.

Interesting. She called Missy, and the detective, as promised, answered immediately. “Hey, Missy,” Faith said, “got a minute?”

“For you, sugar, I have all the time in the world.”

Faith had to smile at that. “We’re at the cemetery in Humble, and I noticed something interesting.”

“You don’t say?”

“It looks like our killer buried Barbara near a relative’s grave.”

“And you want me to see if there’s a Prescott somewhere in the cemetery here.”

Faith’s admiration for the amiable detective grew. “You got it.”

“Right on. I’ll make some calls and let you know what I dig up.”

“Thank you,” she replied. “In the meantime, I’d like to talk to the coroner.”

“I’ll text you the address.”

***

“Both victims were buried alive and died of asphyxiation within four hours of burial,” the coroner explained. “Aside from the petechial hemorrhaging and darkening of the skin consistent with such a death, there are defensive wounds on both victims' hands and legs, particularly the fingers and palms. Most of the defensive injuries were sustained in the moments prior to death."

"They panicked," Michael summarized.

"Yes," the coroner replied.

Dr. Frank Richmond was a softspoken bookish man of maybe forty-five with wire-rimmed glasses and a short goatee. Faith thought he looked like a villain from an old spy movie, but he had a ready smile and kind eyes, and she decided she liked him well enough.

"Have the families been notified?" Faith asked.

"Yes," Dr. Richmond replied. "They were notified yesterday and informed that they should expect a call from investigators."

"We'll talk to them," Michael said. "Any sign of intoxication? Any needle or ligature marks?"

Faith knew Michael was thinking about how the victims were transported to the graves. If the killer was working alone, and Faith believed he was, then the victims would have had to be unconscious until they were brought to the grave.

"There were traces of gamma hydroxybutyrate and flunitrazepam in both their systems. GHB and Rohypnol in English."

"Date-rape drugs," Faith commented.

"Yes."

"Administered orally, I'm guessing?" Michael asked.

Dr. Richmond nodded. "That's correct. Of note is the fact that the dosing appeared to be tailored to the victims' weight."

"He wanted them to remain alive until he could bury them," Faith surmised.

"Could he have a medical background?" Michael asked.

"Possibly," Dr. Richmond said, "but I personally feel he would have chosen one drug or the other in that case, not both."

"I agree," Faith said. "He used both drugs as a failsafe in case one didn't work the way he intended."

"How would he know the dosage though?" Michael asked. "That's not common knowledge."

"You can find anything out on the Internet," Faith countered, "but the victims are both medical professionals, so we'll explore that angle too." To Dr. Richmond, she said, "Anything else we should know about the victims?"

He lifted his hands and let them drop. "Not really. You have their vital info already. I'm sure the families can tell you more, but medically, this is as easy a pair of autopsies as I've ever had." He chuckled mirthlessly. "Not a good thing in this case, I suppose."

"Keep us posted if you find anything, Doc," Michael said.

"Will do." Dr. Richmond stooped and ruffled Turk's fur. "Go catch us some bad guys, eh, boy?"

Turk barked seriously and Richmond smiled. "I had a German shepherd when I was a kid. Great dog. Used to go everywhere with me."

"He's a good boy," Faith agreed with a smile.

Dr. Richmond stood and shook hers and Michael's hand. "Good luck, Special Agents. If I can help you with anything else, please let me know."

They had just reached their car when Faith's phone rang. It was Missy.

"I don't know if it's in good taste to say I'm the bearer of good news," the detective said, "but I'm the bearer of helpful news, at least."

"You found something?"

"Three somethings," Missy confirmed. "Or someones to be more accurate. All Prescotts and all buried at the Houston Hillside Memorial Cemetery. Looks like our killer might have some personal connection to the victims."

"But who?" Faith asked. "Who would know both of them?"

"Hell if I know," Missy replied. "I'll start working on a list of people at each cemetery who might have night access and access to vehicles and gravedigging equipment. I'd let Humble PD take care of the Humble cemetery, but I think you've noticed that they're not very helpful."

"We've noticed," Faith replied. "We'll go talk to the families and see if we can learn anything on that end."

"Good luck, sugar."

Faith smiled again. "Thanks, Missy. You too."

She hung up and Michael said, "Prescotts at the Houston place?"

"Yep. He's burying people near their families."

"What a peach," Michael said. "What do you think about the medical angle? If he's burying them next to their families, he must know them, right?"

"Not necessarily, but it's likely," Faith said. "The problem is that the victims worked in different places. Barbara Ames was a doctor at Houston Regional and Prescott was a paramedic with the fire department. They might have interacted with the same people, but that could be hundreds of people. Even thousands. We need to find a closer connection, something more meaningful."

"Hmm," Michael said. "Well, we'll talk to the families. Maybe they'll know something we don't."

"That's the hope," Faith agreed.

"Where to?" Michael asked.

Faith looked at the info the coroner provided. "Looks like Ames's family is closer. They live in Kingwood. It's a master-planned community a few miles northeast of here."

"Kingwood it is," Michael replied.

Kingwood was one of those unusual enclaves that sometimes existed in low-income areas. It wasn't as nice as the wealthy neighborhood where Henrietta Eckersley lived, but the contrast between the new-build McMansions and the homes in Humble was striking. Faith wondered if Ames's family had always had money or if she had supplemented their income with her earnings.

The answer to that question became clear when Janet Quigley—older sister to Barbara Ames—welcomed the two agents inside. The first thing she said after introductions was, "I just don't know what we're going to do. Barbara helped us out with our mortgage and the kids' private school. I just can't bear the thought of sending them to that awful public high school!"

Faith thought that it might not hurt the kids to see how the other half lived, but she kept that thought to herself. She wasn't here to judge the Ames family. "Mrs. Quigley, I realize that this question is uncomfortable, but do you know of anyone at all who might want to hurt your sister?"

"Of course not!" Janet replied indignantly. "Barbara was a doctor! She saved lives!"

"So you're not aware of anyone who disliked her?"

"No," Janet insisted, shaking her head, "Janet was a saint. Everyone said so."

"What about someone she disliked?" Michael asked. "Did she mention anyone that she had a low opinion of? Someone she didn't get along with?"

"I mean," Janet considered, "she would complain about the hospital administration sometimes. Just normal stuff, frustration over scheduling, things like that. Never serious complaints. Just workplace gripes."

“Did her behavior change at all recently?” Faith asked. “Any increase in moodiness, aloofness? Maybe more or less complaining than usual?”

Janet shook her head again. “No, not really. She had a hard job, and there were worse days than others, but nothing very recent.” She met Faith’s eyes and Faith could see that hers were bloodshot and puffy from more tears than simply the ones she was shedding today. Faith felt a pang of guilt at her earlier judgmental thoughts. Whatever her faults, this woman was grieving her sister, and it was Faith’s job to find the person responsible and bring him to justice.

“We’ll find the person who hurt your sister,” Faith said. “I promise.”

Michael glanced at Faith, then turned back to Janet. “Did your sister ever mention a Marvin Prescott?”

Janet looked up at him. “No. No, she didn’t. Is he… is that your suspect?”

Faith and Michael shared another glance. “No, ma’am,” Michael said. “He’s connected to the case, but he’s not a suspect.”

“Is he another victim?” Janet asked. “Was my sister the victim of a serial killer?”

“We’re not sure,” Faith said, which was the truth but only on a technicality. “We believe his death might be related to your sister’s death, but at the moment, there doesn’t seem to be any connection between the two except that they were both medical professionals.”

“Did Marvin Prescott work at the hospital?” Janet asked.

“No, he was a paramedic,” Michael said. “He worked for the fire department.”

Faith watched Janet’s face carefully, but no lightbulbs went off. She simply nodded and said, “Well, I don’t recognize the name, but if I think of anything, I’ll give you a call.”

Faith recognized the subtle hint that the interview was over, and a moment later, she understood why when the front door opened and three children—all high school age—walked inside, followed by an average-looking man with thinning hair and glasses—Mr. Quigley, Faith presumed.

The two agents stood, and Janet introduced them as police detectives. Faith decided not to correct her. They said their goodbyes and left their card, then left the family to their grief.

On the way to Marvin Prescott’s house, Michael asked, “What do you think?”

"About what?"

"Do you think Janet's telling the truth that she doesn't know anything?"

"I think so," Faith said. "Why, did you feel differently?"

Michael shrugged. "She seemed honest enough, but her answers were very generic."

"To be fair," Faith pointed out, "our questions were very generic."

"Fair enough," Michael admitted, "but she didn't seem to know much about her sister's life at all. It just seems unusual."

"How much could you tell me about your sister's day-to-day life?" Faith asked.

"All right, all right," Michael said, lifting his hand. "Fair enough. I just wish we could find something useful."

"It's still early, Michael," Faith reminded him. "We never learn something useful on the first day. Nothing we would recognize as useful, anyway."

"I know," Michael said. "I just wish that one of these cases would work out differently."

"I get that," Faith said.

Marvin, or rather his wife, Julia, lived on the other side of Houston in Sugar Land. With traffic, it took over an hour for them to reach her. They arrived just around dinner time, but Faith suspected that Julia wouldn't be cooking right now.

She was right. Julia answered the door in a T-shirt and sweatpants that Faith suspected she hadn't changed since yesterday. She regarded the agents with tired, vacant eyes that were if anything even more bloodshot and puffy than Janet Quigley's. She invited the agents inside and offered them coffee, which they declined.

"We'll have to keep it quiet," she said emotionlessly. "I just got Harper to sleep."

"Harper's your son?" Michael asked.

"Daughter." She took a seat across from the two special agents and tears welled in her eyes. "She keeps asking for her daddy. I don't know what to tell her. I just keep telling her that he's at work. How am I going to tell her that her daddy's dead?"

She pressed her fingers to her eyes and Turk walked over and laid his head in her lap. Julia stroked behind his ears with her other hand and spent a minute or so composing herself before looking up at the two agents. She took a deep breath and said, "You want to know if I know of anyone who might have wanted to hurt Marvin."

"Yes," Faith replied. "Do you?"

She shook her head. "No. He got along well with everyone." She chuckled, a bitter coughing sound that more closely resembled a sob than a laugh. "I almost wish I did. It would be easier if I did. Maybe I could help figure out who did this."

"You leave that to us, ma'am," Michael said. "That's what we're here for."

Julia tried a smile but gave up after a moment.

"Did he mention anyone new in his life?" Faith asked. "Anyone he didn't like, or anyone who rubbed him the wrong way?"

Julia shook her head. "No. I mean, guys come and go at the fire department, but the teams tend to remain pretty steady. The guys he worked with were the same guys he worked with for the past ten years."

"What about outside of work?" Michael asked. "Any new friends?"

She met his eyes. "You mean lovers? You're asking if he was cheating on me?"

"I wasn't," Michael said, "but if you have reason to suspect that, then I want to know about that too."

She took a deep breath and said, "No, I don't think he was cheating on me. I don't think he could live with himself if he ever hurt me like that. Marvin was loyal."

She pressed her palm to her eyes again and her lip trembled. Turk pressed his head against her stomach and whined softly. Julia reached down and hugged him tightly, and Turk patiently endured the gesture. Faith felt a rush of pride for her dog. He had more empathy than any human she'd ever met.

"I just don't understand," Julia said. "Marvin was a paramedic. He was a firefighter. I could understand people hurting him if he was something like an insurance adjustor or a repo man, but who hurts a firefighter?"

Faith knew that Julia was grabbing at any straw she could to make this make sense. She also knew that even when they found the killer and brought him to justice, it would never really make sense to Julia. She had lost the love of her life, the father of her daughter. To Julia, Marvin was Superman. She would never understand how anyone could be evil enough to take him away from her.

They asked a few more questions but didn't learn anything useful. When they heard stirring coming from the bedroom, the three of them left, deciding to spare Julia the awkwardness of trying to explain to

Harper why two somber people in dark suits were asking about her daddy.

They left the house in a much-subdued mood. Faith called Missy, but they were still working on the lists of employees. The previously very helpful management at the cemeteries had decided to draw the line at providing their employees' personal information to investigators, and Missy was working on a warrant.

"It won't take long," she assured Faith. "I'll have it by tomorrow. Businesses do this so their employees won't sue them, that's all. Everyone knows we'll get our way. We just have to cross our i's and dot our t's."

Faith could only hope the killer wouldn't strike again while they were crossing their i's and dotting their t's.

CHAPTER SEVEN

He switched on his flashlight and spent a moment admiring the brilliant blue-white arc of light that cut through the night before toggling a setting and switching to a wide beam. It cast a soft glow over the headstones and he thought that scenes like this made him understand why cemeteries figured so often in horror movies. He could just imagine the terror of seeing the silhouettes of dead bodies rising from the dirt and shuffling toward their innocent victims.

He actually chuckled at the thought of one of his own targets crawling their way out of the dirt and scaring some unsuspecting night watchman like himself. He considered himself a fairly brave man, but if a human hand shot up through the dirt of one of these graves, he was pretty sure he would scream loudly enough that they could hear him in Galveston.

He walked through the rows, swinging his flashlight in slow arcs across the gravestones. Every now and then he would catch a drunk stumbling around and mumbling to himself or a particularly adventurous couple looking for an exciting place to play hide the salami, but mostly these nights were empty and free of distraction. He hated to use the words easy money, especially since it was barely enough for him to pay his bills, but it was easy, and he didn't need a lot of money, so the phrase worked.

He was in a good mood. Both of his targets had gone down quietly. He had to admit, he was hesitant to leave them a chance to survive. It would be just his luck that one of them would actually make it out of the grave and be able to tell the police all about their ordeal.

Not that they would have much to tell. He didn't leave behind any evidence and all of the research he'd done online suggested that the drugs he used were very effective, meaning his targets wouldn't remember his face even if they registered him to begin with.

Still, the idea that they might actually get away terrified him. Not because of his own safety, but because of the chance that one or more of them could get off scot-free after what they did.

He reached the end of the row and turned down the next one. There was a soft rustling to his left. He shined his flashlight in the direction of the sound and caught a glimpse of movement. "Hey!" he called. "Who's there?"

The rustling grew louder as the source of the movement tried to get away. He rushed after the trespasser and caught him a few yards past the row. The trespasser tried to twist out of his grasp, but with a deft movement, he tripped him onto his back.

The trespasser cast wide terrified eyes up at him and lifted his hands to defend himself. The guard shone the flashlight into the trespasser's face and the eyes narrowed and blinked under the harsh beam. It was a man, probably in his early forties, but he looked twenty years older. His hair was caked and matted with dirt and more dirt caked his face and his torn clothing.

He smiled down at the clearly homeless man and said, "Evening, stranger. How are we doing tonight?"

"Man, I was just looking for a place to sleep," the homeless man protested in the thick-tongued slur of the perpetually drunk. "I was just gonna sleep is all."

The security guard chuckled. "Well, this is a place of rest, I suppose. Eternal rest. You can sleep as much as you want here."

The homeless man blinked and looked hopefully up at him. "Really? I can?"

"Sure," the guard said, "I'll bet there's a hole with your name on it somewhere around here. You want me to find it for you?"

His grin widened into the vicious leer of a crocodile. The homeless man blinked in confusion. "You said there's a bed somewhere?"

The guard sighed. This man was clearly too far gone to understand humor. He stood straight and said, "This is private property. I'm afraid I have to ask you to leave the premises."

"But you said I could stay here," the man whined. "You said—"

The guard looked back down at the homeless man. Something in the guard's eyes broke through the haze of alcohol and drugs, and the homeless man quieted.

The guard kept his eyes on the homeless man for a long time. He wasn't smiling anymore. His grip reflexively tightened and relaxed on his heavy steel flashlight. The homeless man, whose name at one time was Leon Montgomery, didn't retain enough discernment to truly recognize the danger he was in, but all animals have instincts, and his was to run.

He shuffled backwards and got warily to his feet. "All right, man," he slurred, "I'll move on."

The guard inhaled deeply. When he exhaled, he smiled again. “Have a pleasant evening.”

The man who had once been named Leon didn’t waste any time. He turned and shuffled away, looking back only once he was past the wrought-iron gate.

The guard kept his eyes on the homeless man until he turned the corner onto the cross street. Then he took another deep breath and resumed his patrol.

CHAPTER EIGHT

They decided to order in for dinner. With no leads to follow until Missy got back to them about the cemetery employees, they decided to head to the hotel for the evening.

"Can you eat dinner in the same room as me or does Ellie consider that cheating too?" Faith teased.

Michael frowned at her, and she lowered her eyes. "Sorry. Bad joke."

He sighed. "No, it's all right. We can eat together. No big deal. It's just…"

His voice trailed off, and Faith rescued him. "You don't have to explain yourself, it's okay. I get it. I didn't exactly leave the best first impression."

Michael shrugged. "It's not your fault." He glanced at Turk, who sat in between the two beds of Faith's room and watched TV. "It's that asshole's fault."

Turk cast an injured glance at Michael, who chuckled and walked over to scratch his chin. "Just kidding, buddy. You don't know any better."

"Would it help, you think, if I came over and apologized?" Faith asked.

Michael sighed. "No, probably not. I think we just need to give it a little time. She'll come around. It's just tough with her ex still dragging his feet on the divorce."

"I get that," she said.

She let the subject drop, having learned from experience that the less she pried into Michael's personal life, the better.

They ordered the pizza and right after Faith hung up, her phone rang. She looked at the number and swore. "It's Dr. West," she told Michael. "I forgot to tell him I'd be missing this session."

She stepped outside and answered. "Hey, Dr. West, sorry. I totally forgot to tell you I was on a case." She frowned as a thought struck her. "The Bureau didn't tell you?"

"They don't share schedules with me," he replied. "It's a new privacy policy. They don't want agents thinking I'm spying on them."

"Got it," Faith said. She didn't really, but the Bureau often issued policies that made no sense, so this didn't surprise her. "Anyway, I'm really sorry I missed the session."

"Not a problem," he replied. "Duty comes first. Can you tell me what case you're working on?"

"No, sorry," she said, "I can't share details about an ongoing investigation."

"It's not the Copycat Killer case, is it?"

Faith frowned. Why would he be asking about that case? They hadn't talked about it in months, and the last thing she told him was that she was letting it go. She hadn't seen him in over a week, so she hadn't mentioned yet that Clark had asked her to consult on the case.

"No, not that case," she said. "I'm still not officially working that case."

"What do you mean not officially?" he asked.

"Well, Clark asked me to look over the file and offer some help to the agents assigned to the case, but it's not an official consult. I guess the lead agent just asked for a fresh perspective. He knows that I was instrumental in catching the Donkey Killer, so he thought I might have something helpful to add."

"I see," Dr. West said, sounding dubious.

"Is everything all right, Doctor?" Faith asked.

"I just want to make sure that you take care of your health," he said. "I don't know if it's advisable for you to involve yourself in the Copycat case right now."

"I haven't even thought about it, to be honest," Faith said. "Not since Clark handed me the file."

To her surprise, that was one hundred percent the truth. She hadn't even brought the file with her. It was in her desk drawer at home.

"That's good," Dr. West said. "I'm glad to hear it."

He asked her a few other questions, general things. Was she feeling okay? Any more nightmares? Any positive developments with David or Michael?

She gave him brief answers that were intentionally vague. She liked Dr. West, and talking to him had definitely helped her as she recovered from the trauma she experienced at Jethro Trammell's hands, but she needed to keep her focus on the case, and she wasn't looking to talk about her personal life right now.

When the pizza arrived, she took advantage of that and said, "Dinner's here. Gotta go. Sorry again about missing our session. I'll do a double the next time I see you if you want."

"Oh, there's no need for that," he said, "unless you feel you need it. Just be careful with that case."

Faith smiled. "Doc, I'll be fine. I'm a big girl."

"I know you are," he said. "I just worry."

Faith returned to the room and managed to put the conversation from her mind, but the uneasy feeling remained. She wasn't sure what she had to be uneasy about. She wasn't having nightmares anymore, and Dr. West might be a bit overzealous, but that was nothing to be upset about, was it?

Still, she couldn't shake the unease she felt. She almost wished she could ask Michael to stay in the room with her so she wouldn't be alone, but considering the issues between him and Ellie right now, she didn't think it was a good idea.

Besides, she had Turk. He normally wasn't allowed in the bed, but she was concerned that her unease and the sudden reminder of the Copycat Killer might lead to a recurrence of her nightmares, so when she got into bed, she patted the space next to her. "Come on, boy. I need a cuddle tonight."

Turk immediately leapt into bed next to her, not waiting for Faith to change her mind. She laughed and put an arm around the big puppy and sat with him awhile watching old reruns before her eyelids drooped and she finally gave in to sleep.

***

She woke early and showered and dressed just as the sunrise filtered through the window to her room. She headed for breakfast, promising to bring some sausages back for Turk. To her surprise, Michael was already eating when she arrived at the hotel's dining room.

"Hey," she said, "you're up early."

"I wake early too," he protested. "The only reason you're up before me is you make everything a competition. You always check my alarm and set yours thirty minutes before mine."

"That's not a competition. I just want to make sure I get a chance to shower before you hog all the hot water. Seriously, how does Ellie stand that?"

Michael chuckled. "She showers first."

"Smart woman," Faith said. "How did you sleep?"

"Without you moaning and whining three feet away from me? Like a baby."

"Glad to hear it," Faith said. "Turk's a much better roommate than you anyway."

She got her breakfast and rejoined Michael.

"Have you heard from Missy about the cemetery employees?" Michael asked.

"Not yet," Faith said. "I figure in the meantime we head to their workplaces and interview coworkers. See if maybe there's a connection between the two of them that way."

"Friend of a friend kind of thing?"

"Sure," Faith said. "Honestly, I'd just love to see anything that makes sense."

Michael grinned. "Now who's being impatient?"

"Hey, I got a lot on my plate now," she said. She hesitated a moment, then decided to tell him. "Clark asked me to look into the Copycat case."

Michael's eyes widened. "Really?"

"Yeah. I guess Desrouleaux asked him to ask me."

"Wow," Michael said, "he must be in a real bind. Desrouleaux normally keeps his cases to himself like an old woman clutching pearls."

"Well, he's been working that case for over a year now," Faith said, "and hasn't found anything. The body count is close to thirty. At this point, even the tightest of asses has to loosen a little."

Michael snorted and coffee sprayed onto Faith's shirt.

"Jesus!" she exclaimed. "What the hell?"

"Hey, that's your fault," Michael said through choking and laughter. "You know I love potty humor."

"I know, but what are you, twelve?" she said, laughing and patting herself down with a napkin. "Swallow, then laugh. Come on, you never learned that in high school?"

"No, I spit in high school," he quipped. "Glad to know I still have good aim."

She rolled her eyes. "Yep. Twelve years old."

He laughed again and shrugged. "Hey, I can't help who I am."

He fell silent a moment, then said, "So you're good?"

Faith nodded. "Yeah, I'm okay. I'm not officially involved. Clark just gave me the file. I'm supposed to read it and give Desrouleaux any notes I might have."

"Got it," Michael said. "Well, let me know if you need any help."

Faith's phone rang Before she could reply. It was Missy. She answered and motioned for Michael to be quiet, an unnecessary request since he had already clammed up and was listening intently.

"Morning, sugar," Missy said. "I got the warrant and the information."

"That fast?"

"Yep. Like I said, this was all just for show. CYA stuff. They had the contact lists ready for me once I faxed the warrant."

"Wonderful," Faith said. "Can you email them to me?"

"Already did," Missy replied. "Is the handsome prince there?"

Faith smiled and said, "Yeah, he's here. He says he misses you. He wants to know if you're available for dinner after this is over."

Michael snatched the phone away. "Hey, Missy, I'm here," he said. After a moment, he reddened and said, "I'll keep that in mind. No, we're going to see if there's anyone who works at both places before we split up. I'll let you know. Thank you."

He handed Faith the phone, then glared at her and flipped her the bird. Missy was laughing on the other end and Faith said, "I'm guessing you got a shot of your own in."

"Yeah, I did," Missy said. "Did he blush?"

"Beet red," Faith replied. "It was adorable."

Missy laughed. "I can see why you love him."

Faith's smile faded. "Oh. No, we're not together."

"Really?" Missy sounded genuinely surprised. "Well, you should be. The way you two looked at each other, I thought you had already figured that out."

"Well, actually we… I'll think about it." Faith decided it wasn't worth trying to explain that they had already dated and decided they were better as friends.

"Don't think too long," Missy replied. "Someone will snatch him right up if you don't get him first."

Too late, Faith thought, then frowned. That didn't come out right.

She reminded herself that it didn't come out at all and said, "We'll let you know what we find. Thanks again for the list."

"You got it, sugar."

Faith hung up and looked at Michael to see him grinning. "Now why are *you* blushing?"

"Screw you," she said genially. "Finish your breakfast. We have suspects to eliminate."

"Does that mean I get to use my gun?" he asked gleefully.

She looked incredulously at him. "What is wrong with you?"

He shrugged. "I didn't get much sleep last night."

"I thought you 'slept like a baby,'" she noted. "Whatever. Just drink your coffee," she added.

He finished his coffee and Faith grabbed a few sausages for Turk. While Turk happily ate the maple-flavored links, she and Michael looked over the names Missy sent. There were more than she expected, thirty-five in all. Most of them worked for the much larger Houston cemetery. Only a half-dozen worked for the Humble graveyard.

But the most interesting name was the man who worked for both. Well, not *for* both, but *at* both. At several other cemeteries, in fact.

Emilio Benitez, 36, was an independent contractor who worked as a gravedigger for cemeteries across the Houston area. Most recently, he had dug graves for the Houston Hillside Memorial Cemetery and the Humble Memorial Lawn.

And ten years ago, he had been arrested for aggravated assault with grievous bodily injury.

"Looks like we found our first suspect," Michael said.

"I think you're right, Prince Charmless," Faith replied.

Michael ignored the jibe and took down Benitez's phone and address.

Faith looked over at Turk and said, "Come on, boy. Finish your sausages and let's go."

CHAPTER NINE

"Got it," Faith said. "Thank you, I appreciate it. No, that's all right. I'll call back later."

She hung up and said, "He's digging a grave at a cemetery in Bellaire right now."

"Where's that?"

"About ten minutes away," Faith said. "Close to the city proper."

"Address?"

Faith gave it, and Michael punched it into the GPS. "Well, it *would* be ten minutes away," he said, "in no traffic. We're looking at twenty this time of the morning."

"I'm sure he'll still be there in twenty minutes," Faith said. "Unless his secretary calls him anyway, and he gets suspicious and bolts."

"Well, if he does, I guess that's a good sign he's guilty."

"We'll find out."

They rode in silence for a minute or two. Then Faith wondered aloud. "Spitballing here, but what if he's picking his victims based on the gravestones he finds at the cemeteries and not the other way around?"

"Like he's just reading gravestones and looking up living relatives to kill?"

"Yeah. It's crazy, but killers usually are."

"That would be a convenient answer to the lack of a connection between victims," Michael said. "But it seems a little too convenient. And it doesn't fit with the elaborate setup with the bell and the recorded message. People don't psychologically torture random victims."

"The Demon of Morgan County did," Faith reminded him.

Michael shook his head. "No, he had reasons to choose the women he did. They were whores in his eyes, remember? Maybe there's no logical connection between this killer's victims, but I find it unlikely that there's no connection at all and this guy's just randomly picking people to torture."

"It could be his idea of a test. He gives them a chance to escape. A slim chance, of course, but a chance nonetheless. Maybe it's like the Vampire case and this guy's waiting to see if anyone will notice the victims, but he's actually giving them a chance to survive instead of just propping up their dead bodies."

"Could be," Michael allowed. He glanced sideways at her. "Since when did you start calling these guys by their nicknames?"

She shrugged. "I don't know. I didn't think about it. Do you want me to stop?"

"No," he said, "I just haven't heard you use them before."

"Well, anyway, I was just spitballing," she said.

"No, it's a valid thought," he said. "We can look into it after we talk to this guy. Of course, we might get lucky and not need to look into it."

"Fingers crossed," Faith agreed.

They reached the cemetery a few minutes later and found Benitez working on a new grave. He was sitting in the cockpit of a backhoe, and Faith noticed that it was one of the electric models Missy had talked about.

And it was very quiet. Although it wasn't actively digging at the time, Faith noted, so maybe it was noisier when it was at work.

Benitez shut the machine off when the agents approached. He got down carefully, grimacing a little, and stood a few yards ahead of the grave, arms folded across his chest.

Turk trotted ahead of them, and Benitez started when the big dog approached him.

"Stand down, Turk," Faith called. "Be patient."

In the Vampire case, Turk and Faith had gotten in a lot of trouble when Faith allowed Turk to chase down a man who turned out to be completely unconnected to their case. Since then, she had kept a tighter leash—figuratively speaking—on the overzealous K9.

Turk stopped a few feet from Benitez and stood in front of him. His tail switched back and forth, but he didn't seem particularly worked up the way he usually was around a suspect.

That didn't necessarily mean Benitez wasn't their guy. Turk was rarely wrong, but he wasn't flawless.

"What's going on?" Emilio said warily before the two agents introduced themselves.

"Emilio Benitez?" Faith asked.

"Who's asking?" he said, taking a step back.

"I'm Special Agent Faith Bold with the FBI. This is my partner, Special Agent Michael Prince." She gestured to Turk. "This is my K9 unit, Turk."

Turk barked a greeting, causing another jump from Benitez. "Is he friendly?"

"As long as you're friendly, he'll be friendly," Faith answered. "Do you mind if we ask you a few questions?"

"What about?" he said, eyes narrowed distrustfully.

"We'd like to ask you questions about the recent murders of Barbara Ames and Marvin Prescott," Faith said.

He showed no sign of recognizing those names, but that didn't necessarily mean he was innocent. They hypothesized that the killer knew his victims, but they could be wrong about that.

"I don't know anything about no murders," he replied.

"Can you account for your whereabouts this past Thursday night?" Michael asked.

Benitez flicked his eyes to Michael and said, "Do I need a lawyer?"

"Do you think you need a lawyer?" Michael asked.

Benitez looked between the two agents, frowning with concern. Finally, he said, "No. I don't need a lawyer. I didn't do anything wrong."

"Perfect," Faith said, "then this will only take a minute. Can you answer my partner's question, please?"

"Yeah. Okay." Benitez straightened but remained tense. "I was at home. I was up until about midnight, then I went to bed."

"What were you doing up late?" Faith asked.

"That's not late for me," he said. "I dig my graves during the day."

"Never at night?"

"No," he said. "I got hurt falling into an open grave that some *pendejo* didn't mark, and I decided I was only digging during the day from now on."

"Can you describe the nature of your injury?" Michael asked.

"Threw out my back in three places," he said. "Couldn't walk right for six months. I had to have surgery to fix it. Hasn't been the same since."

He patted the considerable bulge in his midsection. "I used to have a six-pack," he said a little wistfully. "Can't exercise anymore."

"So you use that to dig?" Michael asked, gesturing to the backhoe, painted the pastel blue that for some reason the world had decided was the proper color for an electric vehicle.

"Yeah," Benitez said. "That okay?"

"Why are you so confrontational?" Faith asked. "Are you hiding something?"

"No, I'm not hiding anything," he said, "but you guys clearly think I am, and it makes me nervous. How do I know you guys haven't already decided I did this? I mean, you know I got into trouble when I was younger. Maybe you think I'm still that same guy."

"Are you?" Michael asked.

"No!" Benitez shouted. He frowned and took a defensive step backward. "You know what, maybe I do need a lawyer."

"Let's back up a bit," Faith said. "You recently accepted contracts with Hillside Memorial Cemetery and Humble Memorial Lawn. Is that correct?"

"Yeah, so?"

"So the victims—Barbara Ames and Marvin Prescott—were buried at those cemeteries," Faith said. "I'd like to know if you saw anything suspicious while you were there."

Benitez's eyes narrowed further, but if there was a trick in that question, he couldn't find it. "No," he said finally. "Nothing suspicious. I mean, I think I saw a drug deal go down across the street from the Humble cemetery, but I didn't stop to ask."

"Got it," Faith said. "No one else was working there digging graves?"

"No," he said. Then he frowned. "Wait a minute, you think I was like, digging graves to bury murder victims?"

"I didn't say that," Faith replied.

"Were you?" Michael asked.

"No," Benitez said.

Oddly, he looked relieved. Faith knew why a second later.

"I can prove it," he said. "I have the contracts. They're not with me right now, but if you give me your emails, I'll send them to you. You can call the management of the cemeteries and confirm the names. Of the graves, I mean."

"They tell you the names of the deceased?" Michael asked.

"Not me, no, but they tell me the plot and row number. You can talk to management and they can tell you it wasn't those murder victims."

"How do you know you weren't hired to dig their graves?" Faith asked.

"Well, if I was, you wouldn't be asking me if I murdered them, would you?"

Faith wasn't sure if that conclusion was as logical as it seemed to Benitez, but she allowed him to believe that for the moment. She gestured at the electric backhoe. "That thing's pretty quiet, huh?"

He chuckled. "No, not really."

"No?" Faith was genuinely stunned. "Quieter than a diesel engine, right?"

"I mean, when you're driving, yeah," he said, "but the digger's loud as hell. That's why I gotta wear those." He gestured at the pair of headphones sitting on the driver's seat.

Faith glanced at Michael. "How much noise are we talking about?" she asked.

"I'll show you if you want," he said.

Faith gestured for him to go ahead, then called Turk over.

Benitez climbed up into the cockpit and put his headset on. He gave the two agents a thumbs-up and started the machine.

The motors engaged with a soft whine, but it wasn't the motors that threw a massive wrench into their working theory of the case. He positioned the shovel in front of the grave and as soon as the shovel began to move, a sharp, insistent buzzing whine started.

Faith and Michael watched numbly as the noise attracted glances from across the cemetery. The streetlight at the corner turned red and a driver glanced out the window toward the noise.

Benitez scooped a load of dirt and dropped it on top of the growing pile next to the grave. He shut the loader down and Faith realized glumly that her ears were ringing. There was no chance that someone could have dug that grave with a machine and not be heard, even at night.

He stepped down, once more grimacing as he favored his hurt back, and set his headphones on the driver's seat again. "See?" he said. "Can't hear shit over it."

Either he knew he was off the hook as a suspect or he was just happy to gripe to someone about work, but his animosity was gone, and he wore a half-smile as he approached the two agents. "It's no big deal to me," he said, "I usually just listen to music while I work. I feel bad for everyone who has to hear it, though. I don't get as much work as I used, to having to dig during the day, but I get enough to pay the bills, and since I'm not giving half of it to my boss anymore, it all works out."

"Could someone dig a grave without this equipment?" Michael asked. "In one night, I mean."

"Sure, they could," Benitez said. "I used to do it. I mean, it was me and one other guy for liability reasons, but I could have done it myself when I was young and tough. You gotta be in real good shape, though, you know what I mean? You gotta lift, and you gotta run. You need a strong heart."

"But it's conceivable that someone could bury a body in one night by themselves," Faith asked.

"Yeah, it's possible. Between you and me, there are only a few guys who can do it, but it's not unheard of."

"You know anyone else who can?" Michael asked.

He shook his head. "I was the only one on my crew who could," he said proudly, "but if I could do it, I'm sure someone else could. Not sure why you'd want to do it at a cemetery, though. If I were gonna kill someone, I wouldn't bury them in a graveyard." He cocked his head, considering. "I mean, I guess that's not too crazy a plan if you don't know that graveyards are usually secured, but still, I'd want to be as far from civilization as possible." He blinked and suddenly remembered that he was talking to law enforcement. "Not that I'm planning to kill anyone. I'm just saying, I wouldn't do it that way."

Faith and Michael shared a glance, then Faith sighed. "Thank you for your time, Mr. Benitez."

"So I'm free to go?" he asked.

"Yes," Faith said. "You're free to go."

Benitez grinned. "Sweet. Hey, good luck, Agent. I hope you get this asshole, whoever he is."

Me too, Faith thought.

Inwardly, she shivered. A man who could dig a grave, bury a body, and fill the grave in a single evening had to be an impressive physical specimen. A man who could do it between nightfall and midnight would be a monster.

A monster like one Jethro Trammell, who once lifted a fully grown donkey over his head and another time killed one agent and nearly killed his K9 unit before paralyzing Faith from the waist down.

***

Faith and Michael worked through the names on the list, but as the day wore on, they still hadn't found a lead. As the sun settled low in the sky, Faith decided to try another angle. She called the fire department and after a few minutes managed to get through to Marvin Prescott's supervisor. After a brief hesitation, he agreed to meet the two agents at their station to talk about Marvin.

Gary Sawyer looked every bit the fire captain he was. He had the thick mustache (no beard), crew cut, and athletic figure that practically screamed *I lift heavy things for work all day*. He was possibly fifty, but looked in better shape than most men half his age.

Faith wasn't here to admire his physique, though. When they reached his office—Faith declining the obligatory coffee, Michael accepting—she asked, "Can you tell me about Marvin?"

When she didn't qualify the question, Gary asked, "In general? He was well-liked, hardworking, reliable. Kinda quiet, but not standoffish. The others called him Kid Brother because of his baby face."

"Did he ever have a conflict with anyone?" Michael asked.

Gary shook his head. "No, never. Conflict really isn't an issue here. Everyone gets along." He cocked his head. "Well, in my division, at least. Some of the other stations have issues, but none of it comes over here."

"So you can't think of anyone who might have wanted to hurt Marvin?" Michael pressed.

Gary shook his head. "No, I really can't. Everyone liked him. I know that a lot of people say that about a lot of guys, but it's genuinely true in Marvin's case. Here at work, at least. Maybe he had something going on outside, but I wouldn't know if he did."

Faith moved on to the next subject. "Do you know a Dr. Barbara Ames?"

"Ames?" He crossed his arms and thought for a minute. "The name sounds familiar. What hospital did she work at?"

"Houston Regional."

"Ames," he repeated. "Yeah, I think so. She was on duty for a recent case of ours. She was an ICU doctor, but she would rotate to ER every now and then."

"You said she was the ER doctor on a recent case," Faith said. "Did Marvin respond to that case?"

"He was part of the team, yes," Gary said.

"Who was the patient?" Faith asked.

"I can't tell you that," Gary said, mildly surprised. "You guys should know that."

Faith sighed. "I realize that it's typically a breach of HIPAA, but we need to know if the victims are connected, and if so, how."

"So Dr. Ames is dead too," Gary deduced.

"Yes," Faith said, realizing she hadn't said that yet. "Yes, both victims were killed, we believe by the same person."

“I see,” Gary said. He took a breath. “Well. I can tell you the name of the victim and their emergency contact information, but I’d appreciate it if you didn’t let on that you got it from me. It’s technically still illegal.”

“We’ll keep it private,” Faith said. “Thank you.”

“You got it.”

Gary returned with a name, Joseph Campanelli, 19. He was survived by Daniel Campanelli, 44, his father. “I can’t imagine that Daniel killed anyone,” Gary said. “He was distraught, but he seemed the gentle type. Didn’t seem angry at us either. Even thanked Jackie, the team leader, when he dropped them off.”

“Quite a few serial killers seem polite and softspoken,” Faith pointed out. “That’s part of how they avoid suspicion for so long.”

Gary shrugged. “Well, you’re the detective. I hope you’re wrong about Mr. Campanelli, though. He seemed like a good guy.” He shook his head. “I have a boy about Joey’s age. He’s going to school at Arizona State. Football scholarship. I can’t imagine what I’d do if he got hurt.”

Faith hoped that Daniel was their guy, if only because it meant that no one else had to get hurt, but she didn’t say that out loud. She stood, thanked Gary for the info, and handed him her card. “If you think of anything else, let us know, please.”

In the car, Faith looked Daniel Campanelli up in the FBI database. His record was clean except for one count of vandalism and trespassing when he egged his high school football coach’s house after getting cut from the varsity team.

She found something interesting, though. An article from five years ago. An obituary for a Constanza Campanelli, 89, deceased.

And where was the late Mrs. Campanelli buried?

Michael said it aloud. “Houston Hillside Memorial Cemetery.”

He and Faith shared a look.

“Looks like we have our second suspect,” Faith said.

CHAPTER TEN

When he was sober, William Hucksley despised the nickname Billy Boy. No one would know that by the smile he wore in the television ads or the way he freely used the name when assuring clients that Billy Boy really was their boy, and they could toss their worries to the side, but he hated the childish name. Seven years of college and law school while the rest of his friends were losing their virginity and enjoying their lives just so he could spend his adult life sounding like a character from a 1920s pulp fiction gangster novel.

He had never read a pulp fiction novel, and he had no idea if his assessment of the nickname was accurate, but in any case, it didn't matter. The name made him money, and money, dear friends, was what made the world go round.

For that reason, when William Hucksley was drunk, he found the nickname almost likable.

He was drunk often—too often, the annoying little voice in his head would say when he woke up the morning after a bender with sand in his eyes and a railroad spike in his temples. He found that voice easy enough to silence, however. Besides, he only drank on his nights off, and he didn't drive. Not anymore, anyway.

You only get away with something like that once, he would think to himself whenever laziness caused him to consider driving the half-mile to the Rowdy Rooster instead of hoofing it. *Lightning doesn't strike the same place twice.*

"Christ, what a stupid name," he said with a chuckle.

His words slurred a little, but not too bad. Either he was getting better at holding his liquor or worse at telling the difference.

The little voice in his head mentioned that if it was the latter, that could turn out to be a serious problem for his career. Can't be slurring your words when you're trying to convince an accident victim to give you half of their judgment. He didn't drink on his workdays, but he knew that late-stage alcoholics always remained in a state of slight inebriation. Wetbrain, they called it.

He decided he would limit himself to two drinks a night on Friday and Saturday. He could make them strong drinks, but that would still represent an eighty percent cut in his typical weekend intake.

He had little confidence that he would keep this commitment, but maybe if he kept telling himself he would stop, one of these times it would take. Maybe.

He reached his house and reached for his keys, but they slipped out of his fingers. He bent over at the waist, steadying himself against the wall and nearly falling, but managing to keep his feet. His back creaked as he stood, and he grimaced and promised himself for the hundredth time that he was going to lose weight.

As he straightened, he caught a movement out of the corner of his eye. He turned toward it, but a strong hand wrapped around his neck. He tried to scream, but a hand clamped around his mouth. He struggled, but his attacker was much stronger than he was, and he couldn't move. He felt a prick in the side of his neck, and a few moments later, the world went black.

***

That string is connected to a bell at the surface of the grave. If you sound the bell, there's a chance the night watchman will hear it and know that you've been buried alive.

William heard the words as though he was underwater. He felt as though he was underwater. His movements were slow, and his body felt heavy. He could still breathe, but it seemed to take more effort than it should. He opened his eyes and turned his head slowly from side to side. At least, he thought he did. The world remained black, and he didn't know if that meant his eyes were still closed or if there was no light available.

His head felt thick and furry, and his thoughts moved as slowly as his body. Where was he? He couldn't remember anything that had happened. He was walking home from the bar, he reached his house but dropped his keys, and then… and then…

He realized that the voice he had heard was still speaking. *Time moves quickly in the dark.*

The voice stopped, and with it, the soft crackling sound he hadn't realized was there until it stopped.

Where was he?

The question repeated itself with more insistence as the fog in his mind lessened. He tried to move, and this time he was certain he succeeded because when he lifted his hands, they knocked against something hard. Something wooden.

Was he in a closet? Had someone trapped him in a closet to rob him? He could now recall the hand slipping around his mouth at his doorway and decided that must be the case. He had been knocked unconscious and was now being robbed. The voice he heard.

Good evening, the voice began again.

He shrieked and his voice sounded strange, amplified but at the same time muted. He couldn't quite figure out what was—

By now you've figured out that you're in a coffin. The time is now midnight. You have perhaps four or five hours of air left before you asphyxiate to death.

William froze, eyes wide. At least they felt like they were opened wide. He still couldn't see, and now he knew why.

He was in a coffin. He had been buried alive. Just like that movie where that one actor was buried in a coffin and had only a little while to get out before he ran out of air and…

Asphyxiated to death.

That's what the voice had said. Oh God. Oh God, oh God, oh God, he was in a *fucking coffin*!

Panic started to set in, and he drew in a breath to scream, but never released it, because as though it could read his mind, the voice said, *There's still hope. There's a string somewhere in the coffin. That string is connected to a bell at the surface of the grave. If you sound the bell, there's a chance the night watchman will hear it and know that you've been buried alive. Don't panic. The more you panic, the more you use your available oxygen and the less time you have to summon rescue. Keep in control and look for the string. It's your* only *chance.*

Hope flooded him, buoyed by desperation.

He could get out of this. He could survive. The actor in that movie had survived, after all. Whoever had done this was some crazy guy who wanted to see if he could figure it out, right? He had left Billy Boy one chance, and as long as he could take advantage of that chance, he would be okay.

In his fear, he didn't notice his use of the nickname. He began scrambling madly for the string, feeling along the sides and top of the *oh my God, it's a coffin, I'm in a goddamn coffin!*

Look carefully. Time moves quickly in the dark.

Fear slithered up his navel and coiled tightly around his heart. His chest felt tight, and his breaths came in short, rapid gasps. He tried to calm himself, but when he took a breath, he couldn't seem to draw in enough oxygen. He just gasped and gasped and—

Good evening, the voice began again. *By now, you've figured out that you're in a coffin.*

William's strength melted away. He listened numbly as the voice repeated its message.

Its recorded message.

You have perhaps four or five hours of air left before you asphyxiate to death.

Four or five hours. How many of those hours had passed? As he gasped instinctively for air, the last clear thought he had was the realization that most of that time was likely gone.

He was too late.

That realization drove away all rationality. He screamed and scrambled madly for a string.

He found it eventually. He may even have managed to ring the bell a few times before he slipped away, but if so, he never realized it. The last sensation he felt was his fingers closing around the string. There was a soft buzzing in his ears that could have been static from the recording or the neurons in his brain firing a final time.

Then there was nothing.

CHAPTER ELEVEN

"Danny? No, we haven't seen him."

Sarah Walsh, Daniel's neighbor, kept one hand on her doorknob and peeked warily through the small crack in the door which was all the chain lock allowed. Michael and Faith stood a respectful two yards from the door and Turk sat politely, but Sarah, who appeared to be in her mid-fifties, gazed at them with narrow and distrustful eyes. Faith thought the odds even that if Sarah had seen Daniel Campanelli, she wouldn't let on.

She looked back down at Turk. The dog watched Sarah but showed no sign of suspicion. In the time they'd worked together, Faith had come to respect the dog's intuition. It wasn't perfect, but in Faith's experience, it was sharper than that of most agents. If they had any reason to suspect Sarah Walsh of being involved in the murders, Faith might have pressed the issue, but since she was only a neighbor, Faith decided to trust Turk's intuition and avoid wasting her time. She pulled a card from her pocket, handed it to Sarah, and said, "If you see him, please give us a call. We'd really appreciate it."

Sarah took the card with the hand not gripping the doorknob like a lifeline and pushed it into her back pocket. She nodded and without ceremony, closed the door in their face.

"Polite neighborhood," Michael remarked drily.

Sarah Walsh was the fourth door they had knocked on, and her reception was reflective of the attitude of the rest of the neighborhood. It was clear now that they were wasting their time looking for help here. The neighbors either didn't know each other well or knew each other well enough to feel obligated to clam up if one of them had attracted the interest of the law. Either way, they had to change course.

"Should we try the workplace again?" Michael asked. "Maybe someone there knows where we can find him."

"If they did, they wouldn't say anything over the phone," Faith replied. "We'd have to go visit."

"Well, that's what I'm saying," Michael said. "We go there and talk to his coworkers. Management won't give us anything, but if we grab one of his buddies off the record, we might learn where he is when he's not at work or at home."

"Well, we have an idea where he might be when he's not at home," Faith replied.

Michael nodded and sighed tensely. He was just as worried as Faith was. When they arrived at Campanelli's address and found him not at home, their minds had both gone to the obvious place.

He was working again. Not at his job.

They had to find him tonight.

"So what do we do?" Michael said. "At least if we talk to his coworkers we establish some habits, maybe."

"Or maybe they shut us down like his neighbors did," Faith countered.

"Well, we don't know if we don't try."

"It's eleven-thirty at night, Michael. Daniel works in Galveston. It'll be after midnight by the time we get there, and if we don't find anything, that's another three or four hours we've wasted."

"So what? We go to the hotel and sleep and hope he's not burying someone alive as we speak?"

Faith thought for a moment. Then a thought struck her. Daniel Campanelli worked the night shift at a loading dock in Galveston. If he was used to being up nights, then his schedule likely wouldn't change on his day off.

Which meant if he wanted to visit his son's grave, he would visit at night. Few cemeteries were open after dark; Houston Hillside Memorial allowed visitors until seven p.m.

She checked her watch. It would be midnight before they arrived, well after closing time.

"We go to the cemetery," she said, "Hillside. If he's not there, then we'll call it a night and have the police stake out his house and bring him in when he comes home."

"You think he's visiting his son?"

"Or doing something else. It's worth a visit, at least. One more shot in the dark before we call it a day."

Michael shrugged. "Works for me."

They reached the cemetery at five to midnight. Surprisingly, although the cemetery was closed to visitors, the gate was unlocked. In they went, and Turk, not surprisingly, picked up the scent before they saw their target. He trotted ahead and growled softly.

"Easy, Turk," Faith said. "On my command."

The dog slowed to match Faith's pace. With his head lowered and his tail straight out behind him, he looked like a wolf.

They reached Daniel less than two minutes later, kneeling in front of a gravestone. He looked up at the agents' approach, caught one glimpse of the big dog approaching, and bolted.

"Mr. Campanelli!" Faith called, sprinting after him, Michael just behind and Turk keeping pace at her side. "Stop! FBI!"

He ignored her, running away as fast as he could, which was surprisingly fast considering his short, stumpy build.

"Mr. Campanelli!" Faith called again. "Stop or I will release my K9!"

He began to run even faster, a medical marvel, Faith thought. She called a final time, and when he still ignored her, she said, "Go, Turk!"

Immediately, the dog launched forward, taking off like a rocket and closing the distance between himself and the suspect in seconds. Campanelli shrieked when Turk reached him. He lifted his hand to defend himself, but in the process tripped and fell sprawling. Turk jumped over him and barked menacingly but didn't bite the defenseless Campanelli, who fell into a fetal position and covered his head, screaming.

Faith and Michael jogged the rest of the way to the two of them. When they reached him, Faith called Turk off. The dog trotted away but kept his eyes on Campanelli and remained coiled and ready to strike.

"Please," Campanelli cried, weeping. "Please don't hurt me!"

"We won't hurt you," Faith replied, "but we need to ask you some questions."

"Me?" he squeaked. "Why me?"

"Well, for starters," Faith said, "you're visiting a cemetery five hours after closing time."

"It's the only time I can make it!" Campanelli protested. "I work nights."

"Why don't you visit in the morning?" Michael asked.

"I do, but sometimes I want to see my son after work. Is that okay? Can I do that?"

"Not if it means you have to break into the cemetery to do it."

Campanelli looked like he was about to protest again, but instead, he stopped a moment, then said, "FBI?"

"Yes," Faith confirmed. "I'm Special Agent Faith Bold, and this is my partner, Special Agent Michael Prince, and my K9 unit, Turk."

"Why is the FBI answering a trespassing call?"

Faith decided to be up front. "We're not. You're a person of interest in the murders of Marvin Prescott and Dr. Barbara Ames."

Campanelli looked at her, uncomprehending. Then his eyes widened. "Dr. Ames? From Houston Regional?"

"Yes," Faith said. "We believe you were one of the last people to see her and Marvin Prescott alive. May we ask you some questions?"

"I haven't seen either of them in weeks!" he protested.

Faith took that as a yes. "When specifically did you see them last?"

"I saw Dr. Ames at the hospital where Joey was taken after he was hit by that car. She… she gave me the news."

Tears came to his eyes and he momentarily forgot his fear in his grief. He sobbed once and then regained control of himself. When he did, he realized he was still lying on the ground. "May I stand?" he asked.

"Yes," Faith said. "Can I trust you not to run?"

"I mean, if I do, your dog's gonna eat me." Daniel laughed after he said that, a thin, forced sound.

Faith decided not to correct his misconception. She waited for Daniel to stand. He got to his feet warily, hand outstretched to ward off Turk, who watched him calmly.

When he reached his feet, he took a deep breath and said, "The other guy, what was his name?"

"Marvin Prescott."

Daniel nodded. "Yeah, I don't know him."

"He was one of the paramedics who responded to the nine-one-one call."

"Oh yeah?" He sniffed. "Yeah, they were good guys. They did their best."

The opinion was delivered absently, and Faith could detect no sign of deception or misdirection. Her confidence in Daniel as a suspect began to diminish.

"Mr. Campanelli, can you tell me your whereabouts this last Thursday night?"

"I was at work," he said, "Leland Shipping in Galveston. It's a bit of a commute, but the benefits are good, and I don't mind the drive. I usually listen to KHRT. They play oldies and on Sundays, they play the Texans game. During football season, anyway."

He was rambling, but that was typical of someone in the early stages of grief. Now that the immediate fear for his life was gone, his eyes were vacant and unfocused.

Or focused on someone who wasn't there and would never be there again.

"What time were you at work?"

"I clocked in at nine p.m. and clocked out at six a.m., just like always."

"Who can confirm that?"

"My foreman, Jack. He's a good guy. He used to buy model cars for Joseph and send them home with me. Joey liked Vipers. You know, the Dodge sports car with the big V-10?"

"I know them," Faith replied.

"Yeah, they don't make them anymore. I think they did a limited edition model a few years back, but they're focused on their trucks now."

Faith and Michael shared a glance. Michael turned back to Daniel and asked, "Are you familiar with Humble Memorial Lawn Cemetery?"

"Who?" Daniel asked, brow furrowing. "This is Houston Hillside Memorial. I buried Joey here so he could be next to his mother."

He crossed himself, and his lips trembled. "I buried Marta when Joey was only ten. He was all that was left of her. He had her smile and her kindness. I always used to tell him that he got his beautiful soul from his mother, and he promised he would keep her memory alive."

He shook his head. "Now he's gone. My poor, beautiful boy. I lost him too."

He buried his face in his hands and began to weep. Faith and Michael shared another look, and when Turk trotted to Daniel's side and leaned comfortingly against his leg, the last of Faith's suspicions disappeared.

"Why did you run?" Michael asked. "When you saw us, why did you bolt like that?"

Daniel sniffed and absently scratched Turk's ear as though he hadn't been running in fear from the dog only a few minutes ago. He shrugged. "I just saw the dog running at me. I heard you say you were FBI, but I didn't know if you were just lying. I mean, I didn't know why the FBI would be looking for me." He blinked, and as though just realizing it, he said, "I'm sorry about Dr. Ames. She was very kind to me and my parents. I'm sorry for the paramedic too, Mark?"

"Marvin," Faith corrected.

"Marvin." He shook his head. "God, it's terrible. You think you're going to have your whole life, you know? You think *they're* going to have *their* whole lives. You know that bad things happen, but you don't think about them, you know, you just…" He shrugged. "You just don't. When the cops called me and said my son was being taken to the hospital, I thought it was a joke, you know, one of those prank calls." He chuckled. "I actually thought that he was pranking me. Joseph, I mean. I thought he was trying to put one over on his old man. I said"—he chuckled again—"I said, 'Joseph, I'm forty-four years old. You're going to have to work harder if you want to scare me.'"

His smile faded. "I'll never forget the feeling when the dispatcher spoke again and told me this wasn't a joke, and I needed to get to the hospital as fast as possible." He took a deep breath, and it wavered when he exhaled. He shook his head again. "It just doesn't seem real, you know? I mean, I talked to him. I saw him just that morning. He cracked a joke, and I smacked him upside the head." He chuckled again, but there was no mirth this time. "I don't even remember what the joke was. I just"—he swung his arm to indicate the lighthearted tap he gave his son—"and said, 'Watch your mouth, prick.' Then he grinned at me with that big movie-star smile he's had ever since he was a baby, and I thought how proud and lucky I was to be his father. And then he was gone."

He looked away from the agents, his eyes vacant and confused once more. Faith recalled the same look in Julia Prescott's eyes as she wondered aloud how to tell her daughter that her daddy wasn't coming home.

After a moment of silence, Faith offered the utterly useless reply that you were supposed to give in this situation.

"I'm sorry for your loss."

A part of her was relieved when Campanelli's supervisor verified his alibi.

CHAPTER TWELVE

Kendra jogged steadily down the road, savoring the contrast between the warmth of her body and the cool of the evening. The fall air was cool but not yet chilly, and she wore her usual outfit, a tight but well-padded sports bra and an even tighter pair of track shorts. Her legs were shaved, and nine years of consistent exercise and a reasonably good diet had afforded her a figure the envy of most women her age.

Not that there was anyone to notice at this time of night. Kendra preferred nights because of the cool, not to avoid stares, but that was a pleasant bonus. She liked looking good, but thoughts about what one might do with her toned body belonged only to her husband, thank you very much. He wasn't overjoyed by the thought of his wife running at night, but she had a black belt in tae kwon do and she carried pepper spray, and besides, this was a safe part of the city. She had been running here for years and nothing had happened.

She smiled softly as she thought of Kyle, no doubt snoring away like a chainsaw. She giggled at the image of him lying in bed, open-mouthed, a look she found pathetically adorable ever since they met at the University of Texas on the third day of her freshman year. She wasn't supposed to sleep with someone on the first date, but she knew the moment she saw that little mop of red hair and the perpetually confused expression in those soft green eyes that she would spend the rest of her life with her little pet nerd.

She was so distracted by these thoughts that she almost didn't hear the bell. When her mind did register the noise, it instantly dismissed it as one of those phantom auditory hallucinations that sometimes occur.

When she heard it again, it drove thoughts of her snoring, nerdy, but adorable husband from her mind. She slowed to a stop even though she had two miles left to run and listened.

She heard it a third time, and when she looked to her right and realized where she was, a chill shot through her spine.

Kendra wasn't superstitious, but that didn't mean she could hear strange noises coming from a cemetery and dismiss them. She looked into the cemetery, the gravestones lit by the occasional electric lamp. It was just enough light for her to tell that she was looking at a graveyard, but not enough to see what was there, if anything.

She heard the bell again. From somewhere deep in her mind, a voice shouted at her to run away, to flee before whatever danger there was lurking in the dark turned its attention to her, but she pushed it down. She was an adult, a grown woman, not a child. She didn't believe in ghosts or zombies or werewolves or vampires. She was probably just hearing the night security or a gravedigger moving around. The sound that her mind interpreted as a ringing bell was probably just their keys jingling.

She turned and started to walk down the road, but she didn't return to a run. A few yards later, she stopped and listened again. There was no sound.

She started jogging, but the relief she expected at the disappearance of that ringing sound didn't arrive. She stopped a hundred feet or so up the road and turned around. The cemetery remained as it was behind her, empty.

But…

She crossed her arms and tapped her foot, a habit she inherited from her mother that showed up whenever she was confused or conflicted. She bit her lip—*that* habit was all hers—and finally sighed and pulled her phone and the pepper spray from her pocket.

It was probably nothing. The dispatcher would probably tell her, in a slightly irritated voice, that there was nothing to worry about but if she saw something else that concerned her, please call back.

It was only a few minutes. She would call the police, get this off her chest, take her mild scolding, and jog the rest of the way home with a funny story to tell Kyle when he inevitably woke up on her arrival. He would shake his head and say, "Oh, Kenny," with his trademark exaggerated patience and they could both laugh and then make sweet and surprisingly intense love before she fell asleep in his arms.

"Nine-one-one, what is your emergency?"

"Hey," she said, and the sound of her own voice was oddly comforting in the stillness of the night. "Hey, I'm sorry to bother you guys. This is probably crazy, but I'm running past the Sam Houston Memorial Cemetery on Olive Street, and I… this is crazy, but—"

"You said the Sam Houston Memorial Cemetery on Olive?" the dispatcher interrupted.

Her voice was all at once alert, the polite but bored tone gone. The fear which had fled Kendra upon hearing her phone call connect returned in full force, and her voice was thready and weak when she replied, "Um, yes. I, um, I heard a bell, and—"

"Ma'am, where are you right now?"

The alertness in the dispatcher's voice had escalated to tension and Kendra's knees began to tremble. "I… I'm just past the cemetery. I'm on the corner of Olive and Greenwood."

"Ma'am, I need you to stay on the phone with me, okay? The police are on their way."

Kendra nodded numbly. It wasn't until the dispatcher said, "Ma'am? Are you there?" that she remembered that she couldn't see her and said, "Okay. I'll stay on the line."

She gripped the pepper spray until her knuckles turned white and promised herself that she would never run alone at night again.

CHAPTER THIRTEEN

Faith was in a funk after talking to Daniel Campanelli. She hadn't lost anyone close to her the way he had, but she knew what it was like to feel hopeless, to feel that she could do nothing to change her circumstances and had to simply endure the tragedies life threw her way.

She had felt that way after Trammell hurt her. She recalled lying in a hospital bed and wondering if it might be easier to just end things rather than suffer sixty years of pain and uselessness. It was a terrible place to be, and she wouldn't wish that feeling on anyone.

Turk nudged her hand. She looked down and saw his big brown eyes staring compassionately up into hers. She had met Turk at the hospital. He was recovering from his own injuries at Trammell's hands, and if anything was as traumatized as she was.

They had gotten through that together. They would get through this case together as they had through several others. As they would through many more.

She reached down and scratched him behind his ear. "Good boy, Turk."

Her phone rang. She saw the number and a chill ran through her, confirmed a moment later when she answered and Missy said, "Faith, there's a report of a bell ringing at Sam Houston Memorial Cemetery. It's on Olive and Greenwood Street just south of Bellaire."

Faith put the phone on speaker and said, "Sam Houston Memorial on Olive and Greenwood?"

"Yes. Do you need the address?"

Michael tapped the name of the cemetery into the GPS of their rental as Faith spoke and the navigation popped up even before Missy asked about the address.

"No need," Faith replied. "We're on our way."

"Perfect. Units are responding. Hopefully we get there in time."

Michael spun the wheel and the SUV swung around, tires screeching. He accelerated in the direction of the cemetery and glanced at the nav, which showed an ETA of ten minutes. The way Michael was driving, they would shave a few minutes off of that, which meant, Faith hoped, that they would arrive at the same time or shortly after the police.

They made it in seven minutes exactly, and Faith saw three patrol vehicles. A fourth parked just as the three of them reached the cemetery and Missy got out of the driver's seat. Her normally jovial attitude was gone, replaced by a tense and businesslike expression.

Missy nodded, a single, rapid bob of her head, then followed the three agents inside.

"Find him, Turk," Faith said.

Turk immediately trotted ahead, nose to the ground. He searched for the scent, and as he looked, Faith talked to Missy. "Who called it in?"

"Local resident," Missy replied. "Kendra Hearst. She's sitting outside with the first officers on scene right now."

"She heard the bell?" Michael asked.

"Yep," Missy confirmed. "Thank God she called it in."

Faith decided to reserve her thanks until they found the victim. If they turned out to be too late, then she wasn't sure a thank-you was the proper response.

Turk barked, and her attention—and that of everyone else present—snapped toward the dog. He sprinted down the rows and everyone—including the four uniforms present—ran after him. After a few steps, Missy swore and pulled her phone from her pocket. A moment later, Faith heard her on the phone with the management of the cemetery informing them of the situation and asking where they kept their gravedigging equipment.

Turk leapt easily between the rows, stopping at a pile of loose dirt with no headstone in front of it. Even from this distance, Faith could see the gleam of the bell as Michael's flashlight beam reflected off of it.

"Bell!" she called.

Missy nodded acknowledgment and said into her phone, "No, I can operate it. I'll send you my licensing info later. Thank you."

She hung up and called to Faith. "I'm going for the digger!"

"Wait!" Faith said. "The digger could crush anyone buried in the grave!"

"I'll be careful," Missy said, "but if someone's down there, they've been down there awhile."

She had a point.

Faith nodded acquiescence, and Missy sprinted away, and for the second time tonight, Faith was impressed at how quickly a short and stoutly built person could run when properly motivated. She turned her attention back to the grave, where Turk continued to bark and trot in circles.

She considered sending the officers for their shovels, but when she turned back to check on Missy, she could see the detective breaking the lock of a large equipment shed only a few dozen yards away. She bent over and tugged on the bell, hoping that someone would pull in response.

Nothing.

She swore under her breath and tried to do some math. It was only twelve-thirty. The recorded message said that the victims were buried at midnight. That should give them more than enough time to dig out the victim.

Of course, that message could be a lie. They could have been buried much earlier and the killer simply decided on midnight for effect.

Still, some hope was better than no hope, so when Missy pulled up with the digger—a good old-fashioned diesel model—Faith said, "There might still be time."

Missy nodded and quickly positioned the digger. Around the cemetery, lights came on as the surrounding neighborhood awoke to wonder what was happening.

Faith jogged over to the front of the cemetery, where a woman around Faith's age with an athletic build wearing a sports bra and shorts sat in between two uniforms. She crossed her arms and shivered, but Faith suspected it wasn't the cold that had her shaking.

"Ms. Hearst?" Faith asked.

"Mrs., actually," the woman replied. "Kendra."

Faith introduced herself and asked. "Can you tell me when you heard the bell?"

She took a breath and let it out slowly. "Um. I'm not sure. I think… maybe an hour ago? No, not that long. I don't know. I called the police right after."

She shivered again and chewed her bottom lip.

"Did you see anything or anyone?" Faith replied. "Inside or outside of the cemetery?"

She shook her head. "No, I just heard the bell."

"You're certain that you didn't see anyone? Even on the street?"

"No," she said. "No one."

"Any vehicles?" Faith asked.

Kendra shook her head again. "No, this neighborhood is always really quiet. That's why I run here. It's peaceful."

Faith wasn't sure she agreed that running next to a graveyard was peaceful, but she nodded and said, "Okay. Thank you."

"Are they okay?" Kendra asked. "Whoever's… I mean, you think someone's buried alive, right? Like, by accident?"

"Yes," Faith replied. She chose not to point out that the affirmative was true only for the first part of the question.

Actually, it was true only for the second part of the question. The answer to the third part was a definite no, and as for the first part? She could only hope they had made it in time.

"Faith!" Michael called, his voice carrying over the sound of the digger.

Faith sprinted back to the grave, leaping athletically over headstones as she took the most direct route toward the grave. She reached it just in time to see Michael's and Missy's sober expressions. Michael pointed into the grave and Faith looked into it.

She saw a torn, dirt-covered men's sports coat, a large, Faith guessed.

The coat was empty, as was the grave except for the sports coat and a crumpled piece of paper.

"Should I keep digging?" Missy asked.

Faith shook her head. "No, you're six feet down already. This was just a diversion."

"He dug two graves in one night?" Missy asked. "I seriously doubt that."

Just then, Turk barked and sprinted away from the empty grave. Faith and Missy shared a look, then Faith sprinted after him while Missy jumped into the digger and followed.

Faith swore silently, as frustration and desperation turned into anger.

He was playing with them. He was toying with them. Faith wasn't sure how he had managed to dig two graves without being caught and without using digging equipment, but it was clear that he had buried that jacket to distract the police.

Well, joke's on you, she thought, *I have a dog*.

A mocking voice in her mind reminded her that Turk had been fooled as much as they were. The voice sounded disturbingly like the soft tenor lilt of Trammell, and she shook it away irritably.

Turk stopped in front of a grave, but this one had a headstone. When Faith approached, she could see it belonged to Camille Anderson, b. 1933, d. 2023. And there was another bell.

Missy pulled up in the digger a moment later and hesitated when she saw the headstone.

"The dirt's freshly dug," Faith said. "This grave is either new or it was opened."

Missy nodded, and without further hesitation, she began to dig.

They found the coffin ten minutes later. Faith didn't bother to ask if they were too late. When the uniforms forced open the coffin, and one of them immediately turned away and vomited, she knew the answer.

Someone tapped her shoulder, and she turned to see Michael staring at her grimly. He handed her a piece of paper, the one crumpled at the bottom of the first grave.

Faith unfolded it and when she read the note, her blood began to boil.

Gotcha!

***

Faith and Michael sat dejectedly next to the grave while Missy talked on the phone with the Andersons, informing them of the desecration. Turk sat at Faith's feet, his tail thumping sadly on the ground.

"He got lucky this time," Michael said. "He saw the freshly dug grave and took advantage of that to throw us off the scent."

Faith shook her head. "No. This wasn't luck. This was planned. He wrote us a note and dropped it and the sports coat into the other grave and buried his victim in this grave to taunt us."

"We don't know that, Faith."

"We might as well assume he did," Faith replied. "He wrote a note gloating about fooling us and threw Turk off the scent intentionally."

"We know that part was intentional," Michael said. "We don't know that finding an open grave was intentional. He could have seen it and improvised."

"What difference does it make?" Faith replied irritably. "He's taunting us."

Michael shook his head. "How the hell did he rig the bell at the fake grave to ring?"

"He probably didn't," Faith said. "Mrs. Hearst never actually entered the cemetery. She heard the bell, but she had no way of knowing there were two bells and only one was ringing. Neither did we."

After a moment of quiet, Michael said, "Let's focus on what we know. We know the killer knows about us. We don't know that he threw the sports coat into the grave to throw Turk off the scent. Maybe he did, maybe he didn't, but Turk wouldn't know the victim's scent, so throwing his sports coat in there wouldn't make a difference."

"He knows the killer's scent from the previous grave," Faith said.

"But he wouldn't smell it from six feet in the dirt. He either picked up the bell or the footprints."

Faith took a deep breath and released it slowly. She didn't want to argue this point. Like Michael said, it was better to focus on what they knew.

"So he changed his MO," she said. "That's the critical point. We don't know if this was an opportunistic change or a strategic one, but we know he knows about us, and that means that he must work at one of these cemeteries."

"So we're back to square one," Michael said. "We've already ruled out Emilio Benitez, so it has to be someone else."

"He doesn't necessarily need to know about you two," Missy said.

Faith and Michael turned to see her approaching, apparently finished with the Anderson family. "He would need to know that some form of law enforcement was after him, but the police have K9s too. Frankly, he would probably assume he's being hunted after the first two murders."

Faith took another deep breath. "Right. So he's taunting law enforcement and now either planning his murders around scheduled grave diggings or just so happened to be here at the right place at the right time."

"Probably the latter," Missy said. "Either way, it sucks."

She sat next to the two agents and the three of them sat in silence for a moment. To their left, the coroner's crew arrived to take the body. CSI continued to mill around the grave site, but other than another bell and the recording device, they hadn't found anything useful.

"Do we have an ID on the victim?" Faith asked.

"William Hucksley, 52. He's a lawyer, one of those ambulance chaser types. Divorced ten years ago after a DUI manslaughter case. The manslaughter charge was dropped, but the DUI stuck."

"And he kept his law license?" Michael asked incredulously.

Missy lifted her hands and let them drop in a *what can you do?* gesture. "Guess so. Not that it helped him much now."

Faith was disgusted that a lawyer could get away with DUI manslaughter, but what really frustrated her was the fact that he was a lawyer in the first place. There went the medical professional theory.

"Have you notified the family?" she asked.

Missy shook her head. "We need to wait for the coroner to conduct the autopsy," she replied.

"Make that happen ASAP," Faith said. "We need to determine if there's a connection between the three victims. Maybe he chased Marvin Prescott's ambulance to Barbara Ames's hospital."

"I'll get Frank to expedite it. It should be pretty open and shut. I might even have it done by sunrise."

"Is the family local?" Michael asked.

Faith realized that should have been her first question, but her chagrin was short-lived.

"Yeah, they're local," Missy replied. "I looked 'em up. Ex-wife lives about twenty minutes from here. The son is another five past her."

"Do you know if he talked to them?" Michael asked.

"I don't know," Missy said, "but it's worth a shot. I'll get that autopsy done and call you guys when you're good to do."

Faith got the addresses and the three federal agents left. As they left the cemetery, they heard the coroner's van pass them. Faith turned to see the converted ambulance turn left onto Olive Street and accelerate smoothly to the refrigerated room where William Hucksley would wait his turn to be once more buried in a grave.

Maybe he'll get lucky, Faith thought. *Maybe the family will cremate him.*

CHAPTER FOURTEEN

Caroline Hucksley must have been a strikingly beautiful woman in her day. At fifty-two, she was still striking, but her beauty had grown severe and gave an impression of coldness that would exist even if she had shown any sign of grief at her ex-husband's death. As it was, she took the news not with triumph, per se, but with a kind of chilly satisfaction that Faith thought wholly inappropriate in front of her son, Christopher, who was clearly broken up at his father's passing. The twenty-three-year-old sat next to his mother, eyes red with crying, face wearing the same vacant expression Faith had seen on the faces of Julia Prescott and Daniel Campanelli.

"I keep thinking," he said, "if I had been there. I know it's stupid. It's not like I had any way of knowing someone was going to hurt him. I just…"

He shrugged, and Michael reached forward and squeezed his shoulder briefly. Turk sat at his feet, his own expression subdued. Faith knew that in his own way, Turk felt guilty for William's death. His guilt was just as misplaced as Christopher's, but Faith felt the same guilt, and she knew it was useless to try to eliminate it. You just had to live with it and move forward.

"I can't say I'm surprised," Caroline said. "William had many enemies. He was a difficult man to get along with."

"You got along with him for twenty-two years," Michael pointed out.

"I was *married* to him for twenty-two years," Caroline corrected. "When you're nineteen years old, you make foolish choices. That was mine." She took a sip of water from the frosted glass cup on the coffee table in front of her, then set it primly down on the coaster.

"He wasn't *all* bad, of course," she said. "No one truly is. He simply was what he was."

"And what was that?" Faith asked.

She looked at Faith as though Faith had just asked the most foolish question ever. "A lawyer," she said.

"He was a good lawyer," Christopher interjected, for the first time showing frustration at his mother's attitude.

"He was," Caroline admitted, though Faith suspected Christopher was referring to his morals and Caroline was agreeing to his talent. She confirmed that suspicion a moment later when she said, "He was quite talented. I'll say that much for him. He provided a very comfortable life for me and Christopher. I think that was why I stuck with him for so long."

"Mom, not now," Christopher said irritably.

"What?" she said. "I'm agreeing with you."

Before the squabble could continue, Faith asked, "Can you think of anyone who might have wanted to hurt him?"

Caroline once more flashed an incredulous look Faith's way. "Of course. He was a lawyer. He was never unfair to anyone, not from a legal standpoint, anyway, but people who are struggling blame anyone they can whether it makes sense or not."

Faith wondered if Caroline was aware of the wisdom in that statement. "Anyone in particular?" she asked.

"No one comes to mind," Caroline said. "When we were living together, there would always be the odd squabble, and one time a man came to his office shouting that William had robbed him, but William was able to talk him down before the disagreement came to blows."

"When was this?" Michael asked.

"Oh, this was a long time ago," Caroline replied. "Fifteen years or so. Christopher was just a boy. She smiled wistfully, and for a moment, Faith saw another side of the catty, austere woman in front of her. "Christopher looked at William like he was a superhero. Do you remember that, Christopher?"

"I do," Christopher replied, nodding. "I was at the office when the guy showed up. He was all angry and red-faced and shouting. Big dude, too. Had to be six-five, almost three hundred pounds. Dad just came out with his hands open, talking calmly. The guy shouted at him a few minutes, then just calmed down and walked away."

"How often would you see your father after he and your mother split?" Faith asked.

Christopher shrugged. "I don't know. Maybe once or twice a month. We all got along after the divorce."

Faith looked at Caroline, who nodded. "William and I agreed to be civil for Christopher's sake."

"But the two of you didn't get along?" Michael pressed.

"Well, we had our differences," Caroline admitted, "but those seemed less important after we weren't living together. I think we were better friends than we were spouses."

"Were you friends?" Faith asked.

"No," she replied with the faintest touch of regret. "No, by the time we ended our marriage, it was too late for that. The best we could hope for was civility, and that was all we managed."

"So you wouldn't know if there was anyone new in his life?"

She chuckled. "You mean like another woman? I doubt it. William wasn't that interested in committing to a relationship. I'm sure he had his *fillies*"—her upper lip curled as she said that—"but I doubt he had any lasting connections."

"What about friends?" Michael asked. "Or colleagues? Any sign of a falling out between them?"

Christopher answered that question. "Dad didn't have a lot of friends," he said. "Just a few law school buddies who lived out of state. He would talk to them on the internet every now and then, but that's about it. He would just work and go home."

"Well, he wouldn't *just* go home," Caroline interjected.

Christopher flashed an irritated look in her direction, but Faith followed up. "Where would he go?"

"Well," she said, lifting her glass, "William liked to drink."

She sipped her water and Michael asked, "Where would he drink?"

"Oh, I'm sure I don't know," she said. "Wherever they sell alcohol, I suppose. He wouldn't drive anymore, but he would still put it away. I thought for sure after his accident he would quit. When I caught him drunk the week after he was pardoned for manslaughter, I filed the divorce papers the next day."

"Can you tell me about the accident?" Faith asked.

"It doesn't matter!" Christopher interrupted with surprising vehemence. "It was ten years ago."

"We'd like to know," Michael said with just enough authority that Christopher clammed up moodily.

"Well," Caroline said, clearly pleased at being the center of attention again, "I received a call from jail ten years ago, on March nineteenth. I thought to myself, why on earth would the Houston jail be calling me at such a—"

"Just the details, please," Michael interrupted.

She glared at him momentarily, then said, "Well, he hit a woman walking on the sidewalk. She died at the hospital later."

Faith leaned forward. “Did he ever receive any threats from the family? Any communication of any kind?”

She shook her head. “No, not that I’m aware of. I’m not even sure what family she had, if she was married or not. No one ever told me anything about that.”

“What was the victim’s name?”

“I don’t remember,” she said. “It was so long ago. I only remember that she was killed, and he had to call in several favors to get off without the manslaughter charge. We were worried, of course, about retaliation, but there was no word from anyone claiming to be her family or friend. After ten years, I can’t imagine that anyone would decide to take action now.”

Faith didn’t think so either, but she made a mental note to follow up on the case if they didn’t find anything more promising. In the meantime, she moved on to the more important questions. “Do you two know if William was ever in contact with a Marvin Prescott or a Dr. Barbara Ames?”

Christopher frowned and shook his head. Caroline cocked her head as though recalling something, but in the end, she too said, “No, I don’t recall hearing about a Marvin or a Dr. Barbara. Perhaps that was one of the doctors he represented.”

Faith lifted an eyebrow. “He represented doctors?”

Caroline nodded. “He typically worked as an injury attorney, but he would represent doctors in malpractice cases as well. He liked to play both sides.”

Faith and Michael shared a glance. They stood and Michael handed the two of them each a card. “If you think of anything else, please give us a call.”

They managed to withhold their excitement until they got into the car. Once inside, Michael didn’t need to ask where to go next. He punched in the address to William’s office and started driving.

“So,” he said as he pulled out of the driveway. “We’re thinking maybe Mr. Hucksley represents Dr. Ames in a malpractice case. Maybe Marvin Prescott is a witness for the respondent. Maybe Mr. Hucksley isn’t just a dime store injury attorney after all. Maybe that’s his day in the sun and he takes advantage of it and pulls out a judgment in his client’s favor. Maybe the guy on the other side doesn’t like it so much and maybe he decides to express his displeasure by burying our victims alive one at a time.”

"Up until ten minutes ago," Faith said, "I would have found that idea farfetched."

"And now?"

"Ask me in twenty minutes."

Michael chuckled. "Fair enough."

***

William's offices were in a strip mall a few miles from the cemetery where he was found dead. It was a low-rent strip mall, but clean and well-maintained. The office was also clean and well-maintained. If William Hucksley once had colleagues, he had shed them—or they him—before he rented this office, and the only desk beside his own was a small, fiberboard affair with a telephone and a cheap desktop computer that Faith assumed belonged to a receptionist. She looked through William's desk and found a number for a Ms. Ariel Bennett, who agreed to meet them and help them look through her boss's files.

Ms. Bennett arrived five minutes later. She was in her late twenties and looked like a ring girl with a toned body that was curvy where it needed to be and perky where it needed to be. She had a flirtatious smile and hair that seemed to shimmer far more brightly than its nut-brown tone had any right to shimmer. Faith wondered briefly if she and the good lawyer had been more than just associates, but she detected only a token amount of grief in Ms. Bennett's demeanor and decided that probably wasn't the case.

Ms. Bennett let them into the computer system and navigated to the requested file. "I can't believe Jerry would do that. He seemed like such a nice old man." She thought for a moment, then said, "I mean, we *did* represent Dr. Ames against him, but still, he doesn't seem the type to hurt a fly."

Her eyes widened, and she looked at Faith. "You don't think *I'm* in danger, do you?"

"It's not likely," Michael said while Faith leafed through the file, "but you should avoid leaving your house at night, and when you do go out, you should stay with friends if possible. Do you live alone?"

"With my wife," she said.

Well, that answered the question about a relationship between William and Ariel. "I don't think you're in any kind of danger," Michael said. "We don't know for sure that Mr.… Jerry, you said?"

Ariel nodded, her hair bouncing prettily. "Jeremiah Hunt. I remember because he sounded like a mountain man. He must have looked like one too, back in the day. He's older now."

"Did you interact with Mr. Hunt?" Faith asked.

"No, I only saw the pictures. He just seemed like such a nice old man. I felt really bad about taking money from him like that." She lifted her hands. "But that's the way it happens sometimes. Besides, the side effects weren't Dr. Ames's fault. That's what Billy said, anyway."

Faith finished scanning the file and handed it to Michael. She smiled at Ariel and said, "Thank you for your help, Ms. Bennett. You're free to go now. We'll contact you if we have any further questions."

Ms. Bennett nodded and said, "I feel really bad for Christopher. That's Billy's son. They had a great relationship, even though he took his mom's side in the divorce. I hope he's doing okay. Maybe I should go see him. I'll ask Tina if she can bake some cookies."

"Maybe," Faith said. "Come on, I'll walk you to your car."

Ms. Bennett continued to prattle as Faith walked her to the car. Faith thought wryly that Tina must have married her for her looks. She felt a touch of guilt at the thought, but she forgot about it the moment she walked back inside and saw Michael smiling.

"Everything we hoped?" she asked.

"Well, it's too soon to tell," he said, "and considering the setbacks we've suffered so far, I don't want to get my hopes up, but we definitely have a suspect."

Faith nodded. "I agree. He's a little on the older side, but he's got motive, he's connected to all three victims, and get this, he used to work as a funeral home director that contracted with all three cemeteries where the victims were found."

"I got it," Michael said, lifting the file. "Shall we go talk to him?"

"Lead the way," Faith said, gesturing to the door.

CHAPTER FIFTEEN

"Another shocking development in the case of the Gravedigger killings when a third victim, fifty-two-year-old William Hucksley of Bellaire, was found buried in the Sam Houston Memorial Cemetery. Police have refused to share details with the media about the ongoing investigation, but observers in the neighborhood observed the police frantically digging up two different graves at the cemetery in an ultimately futile attempt to save Hucksley's life."

The news anchor continued to rattle off details about the story. He sipped his coffee and listened for any sign that the police were on his trail. There weren't any, but if they were being tight-lipped like the media was saying, then they could very well have a lead and simply be keeping it close to their chest. It would be the intelligent thing to do, relative to their worldview, at least.

The open grave was a lucky chance. He knew he was running out of room to operate. If they had figured out that he was burying his targets in the cemeteries where their families were buried, then he could be in real trouble. His only hope was that they didn't put two and two together and figure out who his next target was or the game was probably up.

It was cheesy and frankly annoying that he had to resort to trickery like the note and the jacket, but if he could throw them off the trail briefly, he might be able to get the last one done without putting himself at unnecessary risk.

He felt a rush of annoyance and turned the TV off. Why were they digging them up? They were supposed to be laid to rest. It was obscene. They deserved their deaths, but there was no need to desecrate their graves like that. It was just disgusting.

And what if they found his next target before she died? They were given a chance to escape, yes, but it had to be fair. They didn't deserve any extra help. The bell was supposed to be a fair test of whether they deserved to die or not. If they deserved to live, then God would move the hearts of others to help them. The cops weren't supposed to be snooping around with dogs giving them an unfair advantage, an advantage Mandy never had.

A voice in his head reminded him that someone actually *had* heard William Hucksley's bell and called the police, which, the voice pointed out, was fair and within the rules.

He dismissed the voice irritably. That wasn't the same.

How exactly is it not the same? the voice asked drily, and now it sounded like his mother.

"It just *isn't*!" he shouted.

He took a deep breath, then another, then another, forcing himself to calm. He would gain nothing by being angry.

And he wasn't angry. He needed to acknowledge that. He wasn't angry, he was afraid. The police were getting closer, and he was afraid of getting caught, afraid most of all that one of his targets would be freed.

They didn't deserve to live. He had given them a chance, but they weren't supposed to take it. They weren't supposed to find the way out. They were supposed to die, and while they were dying, they were supposed to think about the fact that they had never even given his sister the slightest chance.

He supposed that made him a murderer. Before now, he had thought of himself as an angel of justice, but he supposed that since he wanted so badly for the hammer of justice to fall his way, he might as well admit that justice wasn't what he wanted but vengeance.

Well, so be it. They had taken his sister from him. They deserved what was coming.

With that admission came a decision.

This time, there would be no bell. There would be no message either. He would bury his target alive, but there wouldn't be even the slightest inkling of hope. She would die, and she would spend the last hours of her life knowing she was dying, and there would be no one to save her.

He would buy a headstone too. Just a cheap plastic knockoff like people used for Halloween decorations. It wouldn't disguise the grave forever, but it would at least give him a chance to get the job done without risking losing his target.

He still hated that they were being exhumed. Death was supposed to be a release from sin, an absolution. While these people were alive, they were targets, but once they were dead, they deserved their peace.

Maybe his last target would be lucky. Maybe not.

He took a deep breath and stood, then headed to his room to dress. This time, he wouldn't wait until nightfall. He would take advantage of the opportunity fate had presented him, and he would finish the job he had started three weeks ago.

CHAPTER SIXTEEN

Jeremiah Hunt lived in the Sunny Acres Trailer Park. Faith wondered idly how many trailer parks had such hilariously upbeat names as Sunny Acres and how many of the residents actually felt cheerful being there.

The residents of Sunny Acres surely didn't feel the hope the name suggested. The park itself was dirty and poorly maintained, the roads full of potholes, and the only green parts of the grass were the weeds that grew waist high amid patches of brown and gray. The homes were as dilapidated as the park, and many looked like they were only awaiting the next hurricane to be blown away.

They made their way to Jeremiah's unit and knocked on the door. Turk stood in between the two of them, calm and alert, his tail switching back and forth like a cat's.

Faith heard a shuffling noise inside and a gravelly voice called, "One second."

A moment later, the door opened and Jeremiah Hunt answered the door. For a man his age, sixty-eight according to the file, Hunt was in phenomenal shape.

From the waist up, that is. His arms bulged with firm muscle, and his chest was equally impressive through his T-shirt.

His legs, however, were rail-thin and seemed to swim in the sweatpants he wore. He looked up at the agents from his wheelchair and asked, "How can I help you?"

Faith and Michael shared a look, and Faith could see in Michael's face the same disappointment she felt. She held out a slim hope that there could be some kind of mistake here, but her hope was waning.

"Good evening, Mr. Hunt," she said, "I'm Special Agent Faith Bold and this is Special Agent Michael Prince with the Federal Bureau of Investigation. This is my K9 unit, Turk. We're investigating the murders of Barbara Ames, William Hucksley, and Marvin Prescott."

His eyes widened at the mention of the names, and a flash of fear crossed his face. His eyes flicked to the left and he said, "Well, I don't know anything about that."

Faith's hope rekindled slightly. She gestured inside and said, "You mind if we talk to you for a few minutes?"

He didn't answer right away. She and Michael kept their expressions neutral, and finally, Hunt said, somewhat defensively, "Yes, ma'am. I have nothing to hide."

Faith nodded and smiled. "Perfect. We'll only take a few minutes of your time."

She waited for Hunt to invite them inside, which he did with some reluctance after a few moments.

The inside of his house was somewhat cleaner and more well-organized than the rest of the park. Faith noted that the high shelves carried some dust and that most of the belongings other than decorative pieces occupied lower shelves and cabinets. That was a sign that his disability was legitimate, but it didn't necessarily mean he had nothing to do with the murders. They had been operating under the assumption that it was one killer digging graves by hand, but it was quite possible that their killer was using a machine or that he was working with someone else.

Jeremiah certainly appeared suspicious, looking rapidly between the two agents and repeating, "I have nothing to hide. I didn't kill those three."

"Why don't we start by talking about your relationship to the victims?" Faith asked. "How did you know them?"

His eyes flicked back and forth between Faith and Michael, and after a moment, he said, "Don't you know?"

"Humor us," Michael replied.

He frowned and said, "Well, they conspired to defraud me out of the judgment I was owed for Dr. Ames's mismanagement of my workplace injury, resulting in severe exacerbation of the complications and ensuring that I would never recover feeling or movement in my legs again."

His voice took on a tone of righteous anger as he spoke, and his jaw jutted out pridefully.

"Could you elaborate on that?" Faith asked.

"Certainly," he said, pleased at a chance to tell someone else how unfairly he had been treated. "I was injured in a workplace accident this past December. I worked for the Parks and Recreation Department for the City of Houston. On December eighth, I fell from a tree in Bayou Park and fractured three vertebrae in my lower back. I also suffered a dislocated hip and a dislocated vertebra in my neck. Marvin Prescott was among the first responders who took me to the hospital. I want to mention that he performed his job as a paramedic in an exemplary fashion."

He delivered this judgment with the air of a king bestowing a favor on a commoner, and Faith wondered if he was usually this pompous or if he thought it helped his case to seem dignified.

"They took me to Houston Regional, which wasn't the nearest hospital but the one with whom they were contracted. I mentioned that to my lawyer, as well as my congressman. I find it reprehensible that our healthcare in this country should be managed by a greedy private sector with little oversight."

"What happened after you reached the hospital?" Faith asked.

He took a deep breath and continued, "I was seen by Dr. Barbara Ames. As soon as I met her, I was immediately struck by the utter lack of sensitivity and compassion she showed. I understand that doctors see many patients in the course of their work, but that does not give them the right to treat a patient like a simple number. I was in great pain and great fear, and she showed no concern at all for my well-being, either mental or physical."

"So you don't feel you were provided adequate care?"

"Of course not," he replied. "That was the nature of my legal complaint against Dr. Ames."

He spoke with an imperious tone, but behind his grandiosity, Faith could still detect a hint of fear. "Why do you feel you lost the case?"

"That lawyer," he said. His face twisted up, and for the first time, Faith saw a sign of real hate in his eyes. "That snake Hucksley. He lied about me. He lied about my medical history and claimed that I was attempting to defraud the insurance company."

"What lies did he tell?" Michael asked.

Instead of answering, Hunt lifted his pant legs up, revealing pale, severely atrophied calves. "Look at these! Do these look fake to you?"

The injury was real. Very real. Certainly Hunt wasn't lifting any bodies himself. If he didn't continue to flick his eyes right and left between the two agents and Faith couldn't detect the fear in his eyes, she would dismiss him as a suspect, but he was clearly guilty of something.

That brought Faith back to the thought that more than one person was working together to murder these victims. Hunt had experience as a funeral home director working with these cemeteries. He could have been the mastermind and had help with the legwork.

She wasn't ready to commit to that suspicion yet, but she decided to pursue that line of questioning. "Mr. Hunt, you ran the Bellaire Funeral Home and Mortuary for..." she made a show of checking her notes, "...nineteen years. Is that correct?"

"Twenty-three," he said. "I worked there for twenty-five, and after two years, I was basically running the place. Jack officially handed me the keys after six years, but I ran the show for years before that."

"What made you decide to leave the funeral home and work for the Parks and Recreation Department?"

His eyes took on a faraway look, and Faith couldn't tell if it was forced or not. "One can only see so much death, Special Agent."

I wonder, she thought.

"You take a lot of pride in your work," Michael said.

Hunt drew himself up as much as he could. "I do. The measure of a man is the amount of work he can accomplish, and I take a great deal of pride in the work I was able to accomplish."

"It must have hurt you terribly when your injury prevented you from working."

"Of course it hurt me!" Hunt exclaimed. "Look at me! Sitting around in a trailer, living off of government funds. That's no life." He shook his head. "No life at all."

"I can only imagine how angry you must have felt toward William Hucksley and Dr. Ames," Faith said. "What I don't understand is why you were angry at Marvin Prescott."

His lips turned down in a frown. "I don't know if I'm angry at Marvin Prescott," he said. "But he testified against me as a witness. He claimed that the nature of my injury was such that it was untreatable, and the results I wanted weren't achievable."

"What results did you want?"

"What do you think?" he said, snarling at Michael. "I want to walk again! I want to stand on my own two feet!"

Tears streamed down his eyes, and Faith felt a moment of pity for him. She recalled the devastation she felt when Jethro Trammell temporarily paralyzed her. She had spiraled into a depression that had nearly cost her her job and her friendships. It might still have cost her her boyfriend. She couldn't imagine what she would do if she hadn't recovered.

How far would this proud, once strong man go?

"So you didn't get the results you wanted," Faith said, "in the hospital or in the courtroom. What did you do about it?"

His eyes grew shifty again. "What do you mean?"

She shrugged. "Well, you don't seem like the kind of person to just let something like that happen to you. You must have wanted to do *something* to get back at the people who hurt you like this."

"I didn't kill them!" he exclaimed. He chuckled. "Even if I wanted to, what would I do? It's not like I'm going to win a wrestling match."

She leaned forward and rested her elbows on her knees. "No," she said, "but maybe you had help."

He blinked and looked between the two agents. "What are you suggesting, Special Agent?"

"Maybe you had help. You're a smart guy, Jerry. You have to be to run a successful funeral home for over twenty years. You could come up with a plan, a good plan."

"That's right," Michael said. "You know how cemeteries work. Maybe you had an inside man. Maybe you offered to pay them if they dug some holes for you and buried a few bags."

Fear and anger washed over Hunt's face in equal measure. The fear was genuine, but the anger was genuine as well. He was sincerely shocked at being accused of murder. "You have to be kidding me!" he shouted. "I didn't murder anyone!"

"I'm not gonna lie," Michael said, "you're looking really good for those murders now."

Hunt looked between the two agents and said, "Are you serious? You can't be serious."

Faith and Michael continued to stare silently at him. Turk got lazily to his feet, his tail switching slowly back and forth as he too kept his eyes on Hunt.

Hunt swallowed and said, "What do I need to do to prove to you that I'm not the one responsible?"

"Can you give us your whereabouts two nights ago?" Faith asked. "As well as Thursday the eleventh and Thursday the fourth?"

"I was here," he said. "I did my shopping during the day on Thursday the eleventh, and then I came home. I can't really do much outside."

He was trying to play on their sympathy, but Faith didn't buy it. She looked at his legs and said, "I believe that you struggle physically, Mr. Hunt, but your mind appears as sharp as ever. I'm sure you can find a way to do whatever you want to in life."

"I didn't kill them!" he insisted.

"Do you have anyone who can verify your whereabouts?"

"I…" He looked between the two of them fearfully. Finally, he took a deep breath and said, "Look, you guys are here about the murders, right?"

Faith nodded. "That's right."

"So you're not investigating anything else?"

Faith and Michael shared a look. "If you have something to say, Mr. Hunt, start saying it," Michael said. "Because like I said, you're looking really good for at least conspiracy to commit murder."

He leaned back in his wheelchair, and Faith could see him trembling. Finally, he said, "Look, I…" He tapped the arms of his chair and then finally sighed. "Okay. Look, my injury definitely exacerbated my condition, but that's not why my legs are so skinny. Or rather, they're a lot skinnier than they would be. I…" He took a deep breath. "I have ALS. I've been losing muscle mass little by little for the past eight years."

Faith and Michael shared a look, this time of disappointment. "So you *were* attempting to defraud your insurance company."

Hunt's eyes flashed. "You don't know what it's like to have your entire life's savings gone. These doctors, these insurance companies: all they do is take from people. They're supposed to be here to help you, and they don't, they just take, take, take. When I got ALS, my insurance company raised my rates by almost sixty percent. But you know what, Agent? I didn't defraud them. Look at my medical records. Look at my insurance statements. I declared my disease. I did the right thing, the honest thing, all my life. When I got hurt, I expected them to do right by me like I did right by them for so long, and they didn't. Do you know what they did? They refused to cover my medical care because they said that my injuries were due to a preexisting condition. I guess because my lower body was already atrophying, they didn't think that having my back broken was reason enough to cover my hospital expenses.

"I didn't sue Dr. Ames because I wanted to defraud her. I sued her because I'm now almost one million dollars in debt. Money I don't have. I wasn't going to get rich off of that judgment. I was going to be able to die in peace and not leave my children in debt because of me.

"But I didn't kill her. I didn't kill any of them. At the end of the day, it's the insurance companies who are evil. I'd kill all of them before I went after a dime-store lawyer and a doctor."

He fell silent, and a moment later, Faith said, "The problem, Hunt, is that you've now confirmed for me that you have motive. You're desperate. You tried to win some money from Dr. Ames just to survive your medical debt, and thanks to Hucksley's legal skill and Prescott's testimony, you didn't win that money. You have motive and you have experience with cemeteries. It's obvious in your expression that you're angry, and it's obvious that you're afraid."

"I'm afraid because I don't want to go to jail for fraud," he said. "I don't think I defrauded anyone, and I don't want to go to prison."

Technically speaking, he had attempted to defraud the court by filing a false malpractice claim to try to recover money to pay a debt, but Faith wasn't here to pursue a fraud case. His attempt had failed, and Dr. Ames was no longer around to suffer from the effects of a malpractice case.

But she couldn't take his word for it that he hadn't killed anyone. He had motive and know-how. He needed an alibi or they would at least have to bring him in for questioning.

"Wait!" Hunt said, eyes flying open. "Gertie saw me! My neighbor! She sits on her porch sometimes at night. Two nights ago, she was out smoking a cigar on her porch, and I came out to talk to her a moment. She lives in the house to the left. Talk to her. She can confirm I was home after eleven at night!"

Faith looked at Michael, who stood and said, "Will Gertie be home right now?"

"Should be," Hunt replied. "She doesn't go out anymore. She's old now, eighty or thereabouts. She'll tell you I was here two nights ago."

"I'll be right back, in that case," Michael said. "Special Agent Bold and K9 Unit Turk will hang tight with you."

He left and Hunt turned to Faith. "You think I'm an asshole, don't you?"

"We'll see," Faith said.

He chuckled bitterly. "I'm not your guy, Special Agent. If I was, I would never have done that shit with the bell and the recording device."

Faith leaned forward. "I never mentioned anything about a bell or a recording device."

"It's all over the news," he said. "That last murder, the lawyer, some residents saw the cops pull out a bell and a tape recorder. You can call the news stations if you don't believe me."

Faith swore silently. Of course the media would show up and throw a wrench into an investigation. Never mind that this could spook their killer and send him into hiding. Never mind that if he did kill again, he might change his MO and make it more difficult for them to find him. No, as long as it pulled viewers to their channel, who cares?

"I would just bury them," he said, "and not in a cemetery. For Christ's sake, it's only a matter of time before he gets caught. Either a night watchman will find him or a passerby will see him, or he'll get caught on camera, or you guys will find evidence. It's too risky. If I were him, I would bury them somewhere far out on public land, and I would spend more time covering the grave to make sure it's not visible."

"You've put a lot of thought into this," Faith said.

"Oh yeah," he agreed, nodding. "I've thought about killing them all the time. Not the guys who are actually dead, but the insurance guys? Yeah, I've thought about it. Haven't you ever thought about it? You've never been hurt by someone badly enough that you wanted to see them dead by your own hands?"

Faith thought of Trammell, laughing as she screamed under his knife. She thought of the Copycat Killer, out there somewhere torturing others the way she was tortured. She didn't come out and agree with him, but privately, she understood. She definitely understood.

"I didn't do it, though," he said. "I'm already in bad shape. I don't want to spend the rest of my life in prison."

"But you said you have a plan to get away with it," Faith reminded him.

"Well," he said, "everyone has a plan. You guys catch 'em anyway."

Faith had to admit he had a point.

Michael returned then. Faith met his eyes and knew right away that Hunt had his alibi. Michael held out his hand and Hunt took it. "Mr. Hunt, thank you for your time. I apologize for the mistake."

"Gertie cleared me, did she?"

"She did," Michael admitted, "and your next-door neighbor on the right, Tommy, has a picture of you clipping his lawn ornament with your golf cart on the fourth after midnight."

Hunt laughed, his fear gone now that the danger of incarceration was past. "Yeah, I was a little drunk that night." His smile faded. "So you're not coming after me for the insurance?"

"It wasn't insurance fraud," Michael said. "You did try to defraud the court, but that's outside of our wheelhouse. I would count your blessings that you lost and live quietly from now on."

Hunt chuckled. "Well, I'll live. I can't promise any more than that."

CHAPTER SEVENTEEN

Faith walked a circuit around the parking lot of their hotel. There were a few hours of daylight left, but the case was at a dead end. They had no leads. The suspects they had who had a solid connection to the victims had alibis or were otherwise incapable of committing these murders. Looking through the rest of Hucksley's files had yielded no other possibilities.

So, they decided to return to the hotel and regroup. Neither had slept the night before, and Michael was making up for that at the moment.

So, she walked. Turk walked with her, glancing up at her occasionally to make sure she was all right. Faith felt a rush of gratitude for his companionship and reached down to scratch behind his ear for a second.

Turk huffed, a sound she recognized as encouragement, and she smiled briefly. "I know, boy. I know we'll get him. We always do. I just wish it could be easy sometimes."

Turk barked in agreement, and Faith scratched him one more time before turning back to the case.

Their initial hypothesis, that the killer was targeting medical professionals, had fallen through. Hucksley was a lawyer. Their second hypothesis, that the three were connected tangentially, had yielded no results either.

There had to be a connection. These weren't random killings. It wasn't unheard of for serial killers to choose their victims at random. The Son of Sam had chosen his victims randomly. The Beltway Snipers had picked random people. The Vampire of the Twin Cities Terminal had chosen his victims arbitrarily. It was possible, but she couldn't believe that there was no connection in this case.

The Son of Sam and the Beltway Snipers had shot their victims from a distance. It was cold, impersonal. Those people weren't people to them, they were targets. The Vampire had killed people he felt were rude. He would wait until he came across someone he felt was selfish and then kill them and stage their bodies to make the point that people were too focused on themselves and not others. His killings were theatrical, but they were quick. He poisoned them, and within a minute, they were gone.

This killer was burying people alive and taunting them as they slowly suffocated to death. He was giving them false hope and playing his message on a loop so that his voice was the last one they heard, even disguised as it was. He wasn't just killing random people. He wanted his victims to suffer.

Then again, the Demon of Morgan County had a nearly identical MO. He would kidnap women he saw as whores and drop them in an abandoned well, which he would prep by sanding down the last fifteen feet so they could almost reach the top but lose hope at the last moment. The only difference was that he would taunt them personally and not via recording.

His victims were just as random as the Vampire's. He would dispense his warped version of judgment, and to him, no doubt, the victims weren't random, but to a reasoning, thinking human, they were.

So what was this killer's criteria? People taking advantage of the vulnerable? That definitely tracked with Hucksley. He was an ambulance-chaser, and ambulance-chasers were oftentimes little more than con men.

Dr. Ames made sense too. ER bills were often crippling to lower-income patients, and ER doctors could often be impersonal since they saw thousands of patients. It might seem to someone that Dr. Ames didn't really care about their health and that William Hucksley was only trying to con them. It was a stretch, but it was possible.

But then Marvin was the outlier. Marvin was a paramedic, and not even a team leader. Someone else told someone else what to tell him to do. He wouldn't be the only paramedic responding either. He would be part of a team, and it would be clear that he wasn't the leader of that team. No one would reasonably believe that he was taking advantage of vulnerable people. He wasn't particularly wealthy either, certainly not nearly as well-off as an experienced doctor or a veteran lawyer.

So what was the motive? Why these victims? There had to be *some* reason. She couldn't believe the killer was just spitballing, so what was he thinking when he chose them? What factor, logical or otherwise, made a fifty-two-year-old lawyer as attractive as a thirty-six-year-old paramedic and a forty-two-year-old doctor?

She completed the circuit—her fifth since they arrived back at the hotel—and sighed. She cast back at everything she'd learned in the case so far and tried to find any straw to grasp, no matter how small, but there was nothing. Nothing stood out in her mind that could lead her to understand the reasons behind this murder.

And the next one. She knew for sure that their killer wasn't done. That was one hunch she still felt confident about. Their killer would kill again, and soon. There was a week between victims one and two. There were four days between victims two and three. Tonight was the second night after victim three's death. There could be another victim any day.

She needed help. Michael was asleep, and she and Michael had brainstormed and come up with nothing several times already. She needed an outside perspective.

She pulled her cell phone out and dialed Clark's number. It rang several times, then went to voicemail. Clark must be busy with another case at the moment.

"Hey, Gordon, it's Faith," she said. "Hey, I was hoping you could help me out with the case. Michael and I have hit a dead end, and I want to get a fresh perspective on things. Call me back when you get this message." She paused a moment, then added, "When I get home, I'll go through the Copycat case and let Desrouleaux know if I have any thoughts." She paused again. "Thank you for trusting me."

She hung up and took a deep breath, then headed inside. She wouldn't get anything else from walking around and stewing.

***

Gordon Clark listened to Faith's message as he walked up the stairs to his apartment. He had to smile. Faith's news wasn't good, but the fact that she was reaching out for help and willing to admit that she wasn't superhuman was a great sign. She had matured a lot since Clark had taken her—unwillingly at first—under her wing.

He would call her back in a few minutes, but first, he needed a shower. He had just returned from the latest Copycat Killer scene—victim number thirty. Once more, they had found nothing to help them advance the case. He was grateful that Faith would be looking into it. She had the sharpest mind he had ever seen in an investigator. With her looking at things from a new angle, he had no doubt they would make headway.

It didn't worry him that Faith was stumped at the moment on her current case. She always was at first, but she always figured it out. She would get through this case, then she would help them get through the next one.

Preferably as lead investigator. He hadn't shared this plan with anyone else, but he intended for Faith to take over the Copycat Killer investigation after she proved herself by finding leads in the file and doing so without going cowboy. He would make the case to the Boss and Desrouleaux. Desrouleaux wouldn't fight him. He was nearing retirement, and whether he solved this case or he didn't, he was likely done in a year or two. Chavez was new, and she didn't expect to be made lead of anything for a while.

The Boss would be a harder sell. He still took Faith's near-implosion personally, feeling that she had taken advantage of his repeated forgiveness and the endless second chances he gave her. Still, Gordon felt he could convince him. He was one of Faith's biggest supporters prior to the Trammell case. He wanted to believe. Gordon could work with that.

He opened the door and walked inside. The lights were off to save electricity, and the room was pitch-black, but Gordon knew where everything was, so he navigated to the light switch without bumping into anything.

He switched the light on just in time to see the silhouette of an attacker and a knife coming toward him. He moved instinctively, swiping at the knife. He missed, but he managed to get his shoulder in between the knife and his neck, so instead of being buried in his carotid, it glanced off of his collarbone, opening a nasty but not deadly cut.

He stepped forward and shoved his attacker back, tripping him over his heel. The attacker stumbled but didn't fall. Gordon had time to register a few details—male, medium height, athletic build—but he couldn't get much more than that. The attacker wore a black ski mask, gloves, and a long-sleeve shirt with jeans, which revealed nothing of his appearance other than gender. Clark couldn't tell the attacker's race or age, besides a rough estimate of between twenty and forty or a well-preserved fifty based on his athleticism.

Speaking of athleticism, the attacker recovered quickly and launched another attack. Clark parried the blow and launched a right cross that caused the man to stumble again. Once more, he recovered quickly and thrust with the knife.

Ignoring the searing pain in his shoulder, Clark parried blow after blow. He didn't get a chance to counterattack after the first punch. His attacker was just too fast. He needed to find another way to stop the guy. He worked his way back into his living room where he had more space to work. Once there, he angled away from a knife thrust and threw a powerful left hook. The attacker ducked it and tried to come over the top with the knife.

Clark grabbed at him, driving forward and stopping the blow. He pulled the attacker's shoulders close, switched his hips, and tossed him over his shoulder to the ground.

He reached for the knife, but the attacker planted his foot on Clark's chest and shoved him backward. He fell against the far wall and got quickly to his feet, hands up and chin tucked in a boxing stance.

The attacker chuckled. "You're good, Clark. I never imagined you'd be this dangerous. I always thought you were more of a desk jockey."

"Who are you?" Clark demanded. "What do you want with me? Did the cartel send you?"

The attacker laughed again, circling Clark, knife held ready in his right hand. "No, I'm not a demon from your past, Gordon. I'm a demon from your present."

Clark knew then. His eyes widened. "You're the Copycat."

"I prefer to think of myself as the master's greatest student, here to take the throne that is rightfully mine."

He lunged at Clark, but Clark saw the blow coming and ducked it easily. He swept at the attacker's foot, but the man danced away. Clark's shoulders burned, and he felt moisture over the right side of his chest. His injury must be more serious than he thought.

"Really?" Clark said contemptuously. "That's what you aspire to? To be the next Donkey Killer?"

"Everyone reaches for greatness in their own way," the attacker said, launching another attack with the knife.

Clark ducked it again and this time buried his fist in the attacker's solar plexus. The attacker doubled over, but when Clark tried to grab his wrist and free the knife, the attacker fell to the floor, dragging Clark with him. He flipped Clark over his shoulder, wresting his arm free. Clark crashed into his TV, knocking it over and shattering the screen. He jumped to his feet quickly, narrowly avoiding another swipe with the knife.

Clark's chest heaved, and he felt more wetness on the top of his scalp from where he impacted the TV. He had to stop this guy soon. He was losing energy quickly, and he didn't like how much he was bleeding from his shoulder.

He had to keep the guy talking and try to find an opportunity.

"So your greatness," Clark said, "is to mimic another killer. Your name literally is the Copycat."

"For now." the attacker said. "I intend to finish what my master started."

"Oh yeah?" Clark said, circling behind his couch to create some distance between him and the attacker. "What's that?"

"I'm going to kill Faith Bold," he said.

A chill ran through Clark. "Faith Bold? Why her? She's not even on this case."

"She wasn't," the attacker said, "but you brought her back."

"I asked her to look at some paperwork," Clark said. "I'm the one who's been after you. I'm the one you want, not her."

"I'll get you too," he said, "that's why I'm here. But let's face it, Clark. You're small time. You're not all that special. Killing you will just be another notch in my belt. But Faith. She's special. Trammell knew it. He considered Faith to be his crown jewel. He was going to break the FBI's rising star. He was going to take her body, take her will, and take her life. He came up short. I won't."

Clark laughed as he moved toward the coat closet. There was a bag of golf clubs in there. If he could get to one, he could knock the attacker out.

"Faith is going to mop the floor with you, asshole," Clark said. "You're nothing to her. She found your master, and she'll find you."

"She's already found me," the Copycat Killer said, "she just doesn't know it."

"So now, what, you kill me, then you kill her?"

"You, yes. I won't kill her yet," he said. "I'm going to break her first. I'm going to take her will. I'm going to take away her strength until she's begging for death before I even touch her."

"Trammell tried that, remember?" Clark said, inching closer to the closet.

"Trammell was sloppy," the Copycat Killer said. "He was a visionary, but like most visionaries, he lacked a practical understanding of how to achieve his goals. I don't suffer from that lack. I am careful. I am patient. I will take as much time as I need to execute the perfect assault on her mind and character. I nearly succeeded, in fact, until you stopped me. I had Faith on the ropes mentally, and you rescued her." He shook the knife back and forth like he was waggling a finger. "That's cheating."

“Yeah?” Clark said. “Well, that’s the difference between you and me. See, there’s only one of you. There’s a whole damn lot of us.”

“One less after today,” the Copycat assured him.

“Yeah?” Clark said again. “Let’s see.”

He threw open the closet door. The Copycat rushed at him just as Clark’s hands closed around the golf club.

The Copycat lunged with the knife.

With a cry, Clark pulled the club out and swung with all of his might.

CHAPTER EIGHTEEN

Faith woke before dawn, as she usually did. The long rest left her with a clear mind and a renewed focus. Clark hadn't gotten back to her yet, but he was up to his ears in work these days. He had done well enough as Faith's supervisor that the Bureau had made his promotion official, and now he was managing all of the murder cases in the office. He would get back to Faith as soon as he could.

Still, she had to face the reality that she might not have time to wait. So, while she waited, she would work.

She made coffee and sent Michael a text to meet her in her room when he woke up. Turk continued to sleep, so Faith moved carefully, sitting at her table and pulling out her notepad.

Michael knocked on the door. Turk opened his eyes and lifted his head, but as soon as he caught Michael's scent, he lowered it again and promptly fell back asleep. Faith answered the door and said, "Were you up already?"

"Why does that always surprise you?" Michael said, crossing the room to the coffeemaker and starting a cup. "You've known me for ten years. You know I'm not lazy."

"I also know that you're never up before me," Faith pointed out.

Michael ignored the jibe and said, "So what do you have for me?"

"Nothing," she said. "Hopefully we can find something together."

He scoffed. "Yeah, I got nothing either. I think we need to reexamine this entire thing from the beginning."

"I agree," Faith said. "We've been going off of the assumption that the murders are planned and intentional, and I still think that's the case."

"Even after all our suspects proved to be innocent?"

"All our suspects so far," Faith corrected. "I think we need to keep looking."

"Where, though? That was the personal connection between all three victims. We could say our guy has a general dislike of medical professionals, but why the lawyer, if that's the case? We could say he just dislikes wealthy people, but Marvin wasn't wealthy. I have a hard time believing the killings are random. If they were, then why are the burials taking place all over the Houston area? Unless our killer's living in his car, it's much more likely he'd choose random victims from close to home."

"The Demon of Morgan County operated over an even wider area than here. So did the Marriage Counselor in Tucson."

"The entire population of Morgan County could fit into a neighborhood in Houston," Michael countered. "The Tucson case is a good point, but I don't think it's the same here. The Marriage Counselor killed his victims quickly and left a mess. He wanted people to find the bodies. This guy is burying them alive and I have a feeling the bell is there to give false hope, not for us to find them. Now that it's in the news, I don't think he'll leave a bell again."

"No, probably not," Faith agreed, "and I think there's a motive for these particular victims too. I just don't know what it might be."

"So we're back to square one," Michael said.

They fell silent a moment, both frustrated at the lack of progress. Faith sipped her coffee and allowed the warm brew to calm her. "So let's start from square one," she said. "What could motivate our killer other than hatred for the wealthy or a personal vendetta against all three?"

Michael thought for a moment, then shook his head. "I keep coming back to the personal vendetta. It's just the only thing that makes sense."

"Who then?" Faith asked. "We have the connection between Marvin and Dr. Ames. What about the lawyer? How does he fit in?"

Michael folded his hands on top of the table and pursed his lips. Faith waited patiently. She had worked with Michael for ten years, and she knew that his expression meant he was thinking carefully. Prince was sometimes dismissed as a gumshoe, second fiddle to Faith, but that was doing him a disservice. He had a keen mind, and since Faith hadn't gotten anywhere and was still waiting for Clark's input, he was the best chance they had at a new lead.

Michael leaned back, lacing his fingers behind his head. "What did his ex-wife say about the DUI? He hit a girl?"

"Yes, ten years ago," Faith said. "What does that have to do with now?"

"Revenge is a dish best served cold," Michael quoted. "In this case, it would be very cold, but if our killer wanted to avoid suspicion, he would want it to be cold."

"He could also have waited to be ready," Faith said. "He might not have felt like he could accomplish the killings back then, so he could have decided to be patient and work out his plan first."

"That would be the logical thing to do," Michael agreed. "Take his time, figure out a plan, then go after his victims when he knew he had the chance to get away with it."

"Or to get it done," Faith said. "It might be more important to him to kill the people he sees as responsible for the girl's death than to keep his freedom after it's done."

"So he wants the lawyer because obviously he's the guy who hit the girl," Michael said, "but why the paramedic and the doctor? They worked their asses off to save her."

"He might not see it that way. If he's a loved one, and I think it's safe to assume he is, then he would have blinders on. He wouldn't see a hospital full of people at death's door, he'd see his loved one and wonder why the doctor wasn't doing everything she could to save her. He would see her quick thinking and her likely decision to leave the nurses in charge of providing care as treating his loved one as unimportant."

"And he might think the paramedics weren't moving quickly enough," Michael agreed.

"Or he might just be upset that someone so valuable to him could be lost and be offended that the paramedics weren't as emotionally affected by it."

Michael nodded. "That's crazy, but so is burying people alive. It's worth looking into."

"It's all we *have* to look into right now," Faith said. "At least until Clark gets back to me."

"You called Gordon?" Michael asked, lifting an eyebrow.

"Yeah, I left him a message last night," Faith said. "I just wanted to ask for some help since I haven't gotten anywhere. Since *we* haven't gotten anywhere."

"*You* asked for *help?*"

Faith rolled her eyes. "All right, all right."

"Shit, I'm running to the gas station at the corner and buying my lottery tickets," Michael said. "Faith Bold intentionally asking for help on a case. I never thought I'd see the day."

Faith swiped playfully at him, and he parried the blow, laughing. "Yeah, yeah, yuk it up," she said, grinning. "I'm growing, all right?"

"Did Dr. West encourage you to seek help from those around you?" Michael teased.

"Hey, it was your idea for me to go see a therapist to begin with," Faith said, "so don't be surprised when it actually pays off."

"I'm not surprised that it's paying off," Michael replied. "I *am* a little surprised that you took my advice in the first place."

"Look at you, trying to take credit for my growth again," Faith said.

"Hey, everyone thinks I'm just your wingman anyway," Michael said. "Might as well own up to it and take credit for your resurgence."

"Oh, whatever," Faith said, rolling her eyes again.

Michael laughed once more, then returned to the case. "All right, so we need to know who the victim was in the car accident. The wife doesn't know, and I think we can assume the kid won't say. I doubt the secretary at his office knows, so how do we find out?"

"I'll call Missy," Faith said. "She can look into police records and find it for us."

She dialed the detective, and Missy answered on the first ring. "Hello?"

Her voice seemed a little sleepy, and Faith realized that the sun had just risen. "Sorry, did I wake you?"

"Doesn't matter," Missy replied, and now she was fully alert. "What do you have for me?"

"We have a new lead," Faith replied.

"What is it?"

Faith explained the conversation she and Michael had just had. After she finished, Missy said, "You want me to look up the other party in the accident?"

"Yes, please," Faith said, "specifically next of kin. Husband, boyfriend, brother, father, son—anyone who might hold a grudge against the people involved."

"I'll call you right back."

"Thank you, Missy."

"Anything for you, baby girl."

While Missy looked up the information they needed, the two agents went to the dining room to eat breakfast. They ate heartily, taking advantage of being one of the first people in line by loading their plates with sausages, bacon, eggs, and hash browns. Both talked animatedly, laughing and joking like old times.

Faith felt a sudden powerful moment of nostalgia as they bantered. She recalled her early years with the Bureau when she and Michael first partnered together. She had taken an instant liking to the more seasoned investigator, and a big part of what she loved about the job was the chance to work with him.

She hadn't fallen in love with him for a while, but when the feelings came, they came hard. For a moment, she thought they would marry.

The feelings left as hard as they arrived, and she didn't feel the same way about him now, but there were moments when she remembered what it felt like to love him and wished that things could have been different.

This was one of those moments, and it was strong enough that Faith had to excuse herself and go refill her coffee to allow the moment to pass. When she sat down, her emotions had calmed, and she was able to enjoy the friendly banter they shared without conflating her love for her friend to love for him as more than a friend.

Still, the glow of that memory remained with her, and she couldn't quite stop wondering what might have been.

Missy called them just as they finished the last of their breakfast. "I got him," she said. "Fred Harrison. The woman who was killed in the car accident involving William Hucksley was Amanda Harrison. She was twenty-six at the time of her death. She and Fred had been married for five years. Reports say that he tried to physically assault Hucksley at the scene and had to be restrained."

"And Fred lives here?"

"Yep. Near downtown. He sold their house and bought a penthouse in the city."

"They have penthouses in Houston?"

"Sure we do," Missy replied. "We're the fourth-biggest city in the country. This isn't the boonies, sugar."

Faith smiled. "I sit corrected. Do we have an address?"

"Of course I do!" Missy exclaimed. "What kind of a cop do you take me for?"

Faith laughed and took the information from Missy. Michael looked up the address and determined it would take fifteen minutes to reach the location. From there, they would bring him to Missy's station. "Don't go to the central station," Missy warned. "You don't want to deal with the red tape there."

Faith agreed, and when she hung up with Missy, she said, "All right. We're on our way."

"You want to get the dog or leave him here?" Michael asked.

"Obviously, I'm bringing him," Faith said. "He's worked just as hard as we have. He deserves to see the fruits of his labor."

CHAPTER NINETEEN

The building where Fred Harrison lived was a reasonably well-appointed high-rise a mile outside of downtown. Faith counted thirty-five stories, and according to the receptionist at the leasing office, the penthouse occupied the top three. Fred had put his wife's life insurance money to good use, relatively speaking.

Faith and Michael took the elevator to the lowermost of the penthouse floors and knocked on the door. Fred's workplace told them that he was out of the office today. It was quite possible that he was out somewhere enjoying the beautiful sunshine, but they decided to try him at home first.

That proved to be the right decision when Fred answered the door on the first ring. "Hello?" he asked, frowning in confusion at the two agents. "Can I help you?"

He was tallish, perhaps an inch shorter than Michael's six-foot-one, and had blond hair and bright blue eyes. He was in good shape and answered the door wearing a track shirt declaring him a participant in last year's Houston Marathon. He looked good. Faith wondered if he had this physique when he was married or if exercise and healthy living was something he picked up after his wife's death as a means to cope with her loss.

Or as a means to get in shape for the murders he planned to commit.

"Good morning," she said, "Fred Harrison?"

Fred nodded. "Can I help you?"

"I'm Special Agent Faith Bold with the Federal Bureau of Investigation. This is my partner, Special Agent Michael Prince and my K9 unit, Turk."

"Okay," he said, still confused. "How can I help you?" he asked for the third time.

"We're investigating the murders of Marvin Prescott, Dr. Barbara Ames, and William Hucksley, Esquire. We'd like to ask you some questions. Can we come inside?"

He stared at them a moment, brow furrowed in confusion. "I mean, I don't recognize those names, so I'm not sure how I can help you."

He seemed defensive, and Faith wasn't sure if that was the typical anxiety citizens felt around law enforcement, or if he had something to hide. She glanced at Turk to see if the dog had any intuition to offer. He watched Fred warily, and Faith decided the jury was still out.

"It'll only be a few minutes," Michael said.

He hesitated a moment longer, then shrugged. "Sure. Come on in."

He led them into a spacious living room that looked bigger than Faith's entire apartment. The flooring was polished marble, and the furniture was all carved from some dark dense hardwood—mahogany, Faith guessed.

"Do you guys want some coffee?" Fred asked. "Or a smoothie?"

"A smoothie?" Michael asked.

"Yeah, like a protein shake," he said. "I usually drink a protein shake for breakfast. I've already had mine, but I don't mind making a couple more."

"Coffee will be fine," Michael said.

Fred looked at Faith, who shook her head. He shrugged and went to the kitchen, a room as spacious as Faith's living room and appointed with expensive stainless steel smart appliances with digital touchscreens. She couldn't find the coffee maker until Fred touched what looked like a cabinet and a screen lit up asking if he would like a drip coffee or a cappuccino.

Faith and Michael shared a glance. This kitchen alone cost more than any life insurance policy Faith knew about, so Faith could rule out the idea that he had used his wife's life insurance money to finance his life.

Not that it had anything to do with the murder investigation.

Fred handed Michael a cappuccino and made one for himself. Michael took a sip and nodded appreciatively. "This is good."

"Yeah, the guy who did my kitchen said it's the new thing in New York," Fred commented. He offered Michael a smile and added, "I think he was just trying to hype it up, but that's okay. I was going to buy it anyway."

"You've done well for yourself," Faith said.

"Thank you," Fred replied. "Yeah, the investment thing kinda became all I had for a while. My wife died in a car accident ten years ago, and I kinda became a workaholic. Well, *she* wasn't in a car. The guy who hit her was, though. He was a drunk driver." A shadow crossed his face. "Fucking asshole. He didn't even serve jail time. Didn't even lose his law license."

His eyes widened as he realized something. "Hey, you said Hucksley? William Hucksley?"

"Yes," Faith said.

"Hell yes," Fred cheered, pumping the fist that wasn't holding the coffee. Faith saw a flash of vicious triumph cross his face, the first sign of unpleasantness in his otherwise rather mellow demeanor. "That's the asshole who hit my wife! Ha! Hell yes! Serves that asshole right."

He caught himself and noticed the agents' expressions. Turk's tail was once more switching back and forth like a wolf stalking its prey.

"Hey, do you guys have any ID?" he asked.

Faith and Michael produced their IDs and Fred checked them. He opened his own phone and looked something up. Faith guessed he was looking for a number to call to verify the IDs. In the end, though, he closed his phone and handed the IDs back.

"All right," he said, "do you guys want to sit?"

The agents joined him in the living room. As soon as he sat, Fred said, "Well, I guess you guys can tell that I'm not broken up about the fact that my wife's murderer is dead."

"No one can blame you for that," Michael said. "Hell, if someone had killed my wife in a drunk driving accident, I would want to kill them myself."

"Oh, I wanted to," Fred said. "When I saw the prick standing there with the cops, slurring his words and stumbling like an asshole, I nearly tore his head off. If those cops hadn't been there, you guys wouldn't need to be questioning me now because I'd be serving fifteen to twenty-five for murder, second degree."

"But that's not how it went down," Faith said.

"No," he agreed. "They stopped me, and I ended up… well, cooling off isn't the right way to say it. Thinking better of my decision would be a better way to say it."

"Can you elaborate on that?" Michael asked.

Fred sipped his coffee and shrugged. "I don't know," he said, "I guess I just decided that Mandy wouldn't want me to kill him. She was the kindest person you can imagine." He looked over at the far wall and got a faraway look in his eye. "She was so beautiful. I remember the first day I saw her. She smiled at me, and I was just… well, let's just say I believed in love at first sight after that moment. She had this little snaggletooth"—he reached up and tapped his left upper incisor—"right here. She hated it, of course, but I just thought it was the most precious thing I'd ever seen. I asked her to marry me six weeks after I met her.

She said no, of course. The first time." He chuckled. "Actually, the first several times. It wasn't until our first anniversary that she finally sighed and said, "Well, all right, if you're not gonna shut up about it."

He laughed, and despite the fact that Fred was suspected of three of the most vicious murders Faith had ever investigated, she had to smile. "I'm sorry for your loss," she said.

"Yeah," he said, nodding. "Me too."

He sipped his coffee and said, "You know, I've been without her for longer than I was with her, and I still can't look at another woman. I don't mean I'm celibate or anything, but…" He shrugged. "I've never fallen in love again."

He met the agents' eyes and said, "So yeah, I'm happy that asshole's dead. But I didn't kill him."

"What about Dr. Barbara Ames?" Faith asked.

"I don't know her," Fred said. "Sorry."

"Marvin Prescott?"

He shook his head again. "No. I only remember the lawyer who hit her."

Faith glanced back at Turk. He still watched Fred, but his tail was no longer switching back and forth like a predator's.

"You know," Fred continued, "I probably would have gone after him regardless of what happened to Mandy if she hadn't been acting like a moron and skipping in the middle of the street like that."

Michael paused with his coffee halfway to his mouth. Faith stared directly at Fred and said, "Come again?"

"Yeah, it was kind of her fault," he said. He took a deep breath and released it slowly. "I didn't admit it to myself for years, but I always thought deep down that it was her fault for being in the street, and if she'd just been on the sidewalk where she was supposed to be, that lawyer would never have hit her. Not that that excuses him for being drunk, but it gets him off for murder, I suppose."

It had, in fact, gotten him off for murder, and was probably what allowed him to keep his legal license.

Then again, hadn't Caroline Hucksley said that Mandy was on the sidewalk?

"You're sure she was in the road?" Michael asked.

"Yeah, she was," Fred said, "the police report even confirmed it."

"So you weren't there at the time of the accident."

"No, I was at home. She was walking home from the bus stop. Her car was in the shop, and she didn't want me to give her a ride because she wanted to ride the bus. I guess she rode the bus a lot before she met me, so it was some nostalgic thing for her. I think she was a little drunk herself to be honest. She was coming home from a friend's house."

Faith made a mental note to look at a copy of that police report. "So you ended up forgiving Hucksley, and you don't know Dr. Ames or Prescott."

"I didn't forgive Hucksley," he corrected. "Mandy shouldn't have been in the road, but he had time to stop, and if he was sober, he would have. He's still a prick, and I'm still glad he's dead." He sipped his coffee again. "But it wasn't me. I wish it was, but like I said, that wouldn't have been what Mandy wanted."

Faith leaned back in her chair and considered while Michael continued to question him. He seemed sincere in his answers. He certainly made no attempt to hide his hatred for Hucksley or his joy at the guy's demise. He seemed just as sincere about his insistence that he didn't kill Hucksley because it would have been disrespectful to Mandy's memory.

She felt a touch of desperation threaten to creep into her mind. He was perfect. For the fourth time, they had a perfect suspect who checked all of their boxes, but when they came to question him, he seemed less and less likely with each passing moment.

"Can you tell me what your experience was with Mandy once you arrived on the scene of the accident?" she asked. "Actually, we'll start just after the scene. Did you ride with her to the hospital?"

"Yeah, I did," he said. "She didn't wake up until the next day. I spent the whole ride begging her to stay with me."

"What was your impression of the paramedics?" Faith asked.

He shrugged. "They were good kids. They were professional. I could tell they thought she was a lost cause, but they didn't let that stop them. They worked their asses off. So did the doctors at the hospital."

"Tell me about the hospital. Did you feel Mandy was treated properly?"

"Well, yeah," he said. "The doctors worked their asses off, like I said. She would never have woken up without their help."

Faith's eyes widened and once more Michael's coffee paused on its way to his lips.

"So she didn't die right away."

"No, not for another three months."

Faith actually recoiled slightly in shock. Michael set his coffee down and leaned forward on his knees. "She spent three months in the hospital?" he asked.

"No," he replied. "They kept her for forty-eight hours and then sent her home. She died in our living room."

"So Hucksley didn't kill her."

"He did," Fred insisted, nodding his head for emphasis. "Just not right away."

"How did she die?" Faith asked.

"A cerebral embolism," Fred said. "The doctors didn't notice at first because it was apparently really tiny when she came in the night of the accident, and they were focused on the skull fracture and the broken bones. She had headaches when they sent her home, but we both just assumed that was part of the lingering trauma. We never suspected an embolism."

"And you know for sure that the accident caused the embolism?" Faith asked.

"Yeah, that's what the coroner said. He talked to the doctor who treated her, and based on that conversation…" His voice trailed off. "Hey, you know what? I think I remember Dr. Ames after all. She was the one who treated Mandy after the accident, right?"

"Right," Faith said.

"Yeah, I remember now. She was really sweet, but I thought she was a little out of her depth. She had *just* completed her residency when Mandy got there. She was my age, and I could tell she was a little overwhelmed being an ER doctor. She was normally an ICU doctor, I guess, but Houston Regional requires all of their attendings to rotate to the ER at least once a month. Guess we just got unlucky that we had the least experienced one. She was really upset about missing the embolism. I had to hold her and tell her it wasn't her fault."

"So you never blamed her," Faith said, hoping her frustration didn't show. "Not even a little bit."

Fred shook his head. "No, I didn't blame her. She was thrown to the wolves. I was a little upset at the hospital administration for that stupid policy, but that's not the doctor's fault. She did her best."

Faith and Michael shared a look and Faith saw the same frustration on Michael's face that she felt. Other than his hatred for William Hucksley, he showed no animosity toward the victims. He didn't even remember Marvin Prescott.

Faith sighed. "Mr. Harrison, can you confirm your whereabouts this past Monday night?"

"Yeah, I was here," he said. "The penthouse has security footage if you want to check it out. The parking garage does too, if you don't trust the penthouse's cameras. My space is 118A. If you go to the security office, they'll help you out."

Michael went to check. While he did, Faith continued to interrogate Harrison, mostly to fill the time.

"You're in pretty good shape, Fred," she said. "Did that start after Mandy's death?"

He nodded. "Yeah, that was the thing I did when I wasn't working. I would get up really early in the morning and run. I would stay up late and lift weights and do calisthenics. Basically anything I could do to fill the time. I had trouble sleeping, and I didn't want to sit alone in my house, so I just kept moving. I would run in the morning and go to the gym at night."

"And you've never dated since Mandy died?"

"Well, not seriously. After six months or so, I couldn't go any longer without… well, you know."

"Sure," she said with a nod.

"But it was never serious. I met a couple of people at the gym, one woman at work." He chuckled. "That was a mistake. Never sleep with your coworkers."

Faith thought of her long-dead relationship with Michael and nodded noncommittally. "Do you ever visit Mandy's grave?"

"Oh, she was cremated," Fred said.

Boy, this day was full of surprises. "Are her ashes with you or do you keep them at a mausoleum?"

"They're here," he said. "They're in…well, you don't need to see them, do you?"

"No," she said, "I was just curious."

He nodded. "Okay. Um…" His eyes widened. "Wait a minute. Is it the Graveyard Killer? Is he the one who killed Hucksley and Ames?"

"We can't comment on an ongoing investigation," Faith demurred.

Fred grinned, but only for a moment before his grin faded. He chuckled and said, "I was about to say I owe the guy a favor, but Dr. Ames didn't deserve to die. I don't know this Prescott guy, but if he was one of the paramedics who helped Mandy, he didn't deserve to die either." He chuckled again, but there was no humor in it this time. "I sometimes wish that we could train serial killers to only target people who deserve to die. Like that guy from that TV show a few years back, the blood spatter guy."

"Trust me," Faith said seriously, "you don't want to pull at that thread. Your wife was right. Killing other people, even for revenge, is wrong."

"I keep telling myself that," he replied, "but then I wonder, you know, what if someone had shot Ted Bundy before he killed all of those women? Is it really wrong to want bad people to die?"

There would have been another Bundy, Faith thought. *Someone would have shown up. There's always evil people.*

She didn't say this out loud, though, because Michael returned. As before with Hunt, his expression gave the answer away.

"Mr. Harrison," he said, extending his hand, "security footage confirms that you were on the premises during the nights of all three murders. You're off the hook."

Fred shook his hand and said, "Thank you, Special Agent. I'm sorry I couldn't be of more help." He grinned sheepishly and added, "Well, I guess I'm not sorry that I'm not the murderer."

Michael smiled politely and withdrew his hand. "Thank you for your time, Mr. Harrison."

"You're welcome," he said. "For what it's worth, I hope you catch the guy. People shouldn't have to lose their loved ones because of someone else's emotional problems."

"No," Faith agreed, "they shouldn't."

But they do. There's always another Bundy.

CHAPTER TWENTY

He waited behind the massive transformer on the first floor of the employee garage. His heart pounded in his chest, and he had to fight to keep from fidgeting. He was out of view of the security cameras, but he felt it was still prudent to appear as inconspicuous as possible. Just in case anyone happened to glance his way.

No one had come this way, and no one would. He had visited the hospital several times since Mandy's death, and he knew that only one person frequented this area, a certain veteran charge nurse who didn't want her coworkers to know that she still smoked and slunk to the transformer bank every few hours to work through a few American Spirits before popping a handful of Altoids and returning to work.

She would probably end up croaking from a heart attack in a few years if he just left her alone. Or maybe she'd waste away from lung cancer, and he'd have the pleasure of watching her shrivel up.

But that wasn't his style. He wanted her to suffer. Not the long, slow decline of cancer, surrounded by friends and family who ensured your last moments were as comfortable as possible. She needed to feel terror, utter terror, in her last moments. She deserved no happiness at the end, and she would receive none.

He wiped a hand across his brow and took deep breaths to steady himself. He wasn't nervous. He had planned this out thoroughly. This was by far the least risky of his targets to kill, daylight notwithstanding.

It was also the most important. All four of them were responsible for his sister's death, but this nurse, this Beulah Ford, she was the worst. She had sent Mandy home. She had pushed to release her to free up beds for other people, and she hadn't even thought to make sure that his bandaged sister who still had a damned *skull* fracture was good to recover at home.

The doctor should have scanned her again. The paramedic should have gotten her to the hospital faster. Of course that prick Hucksley shouldn't have hit her in the first place.

But she would have been fine. She would have made it if it weren't for this bitch nurse, Beulah Ford.

That's why he saved her for last.

He looked up and his breath caught in his throat. She was coming! He watched gleefully, but with a hint of distaste as she waddled her way to the transformer, jowls flapping like a bulldog's. How the hell did they allow people like that to become nurses anyway? Were *they* supposed to advise people on their health?

The voice in his head reminded him that he had looked no different before Mandy died. Hell, he had smoked more than Ford did. There was no need to judge her for her appearance. She had a far more serious charge to answer to anyway.

He waited until she pulled her cigarette out and lit it. She took a deep drag, and when she closed her eyes to savor the smoke, he rushed forward. Her eyes opened and widened in terror, but she had to blow out the smoke and draw in another breath before she could scream, and by then it was too late. The needle was buried in her neck, and her eyes were already beginning to glaze over.

Getting her into the van took some doing, but he had worked out religiously six days a week for the past ten years, and if he could dig a grave and lower a coffin into the ground and then fill the grave in one night, then he could handle a big woman.

He got her into the van, taking care to make sure she was securely positioned and safe from too much jostling. It wouldn't do to have her die on the way from rolling around the back of the van.

He got into the van and pulled smoothly out of the parking lot. The security officer nodded to him as he left, and he lifted a hand in farewell before pulling out onto the road.

The sun was an inch or two above the horizon. By the time he reached his destination, it would be brunch time. That gave him a good nine hours of daylight to work with.

More than enough.

He pulled onto the 69 freeway and accelerated to a smooth and steady sixty-five. He briefly considered allowing Beulah to see him before he buried her. He could do that if he wanted. She could scream all she wanted. No one had been to the Church of Galilee in thirty years. The cemetery was barely recognizable as a cemetery.

But that's where old Charles and Emily Cartwright had been buried. It was only right that their granddaughter join them in her rest.

He smiled as he thought of Beulah arriving in Heaven to her grandparents' open arms. He was truly a compassionate man allowing her the chance to do that. Mandy had been cremated, but that was okay. She was with her husband. He had hoped to be buried next to his sister when he died himself, but Fred was a good man, and he made Mandy happy. He deserved to keep her near, and she would have been pleased to know he still loved her after all these years.

Death had always fascinated him. Not in a medical sense. That was pretty self-explanatory. When your neurons stopped firing and your heart stopped pumping, you were dead. The afterlife didn't fascinate him much either. After many years of doubt, he had decided that God probably did exist, and that Heaven and Hell, or some version of them, probably existed as well. It just made more sense than to believe that all of existence was just a random accident. Still, what happened after death was unknown and unknowable, and something that was unknowable wasn't worth his time or energy to explore.

But the way the living approached death, that fascinated him. When he taught history at the university, he would always dedicate one class to the subject.

In the Western world, burial was by far the most common final arrangement. His targets' families preferred burial, and out of respect for them, he chose the same final arrangement. Cremation was a distant but still fairly common second in the Western world, but in other cultures, such as traditional Hindu culture, cremation was preferred.

He looked out the window where a small flock of turkey vultures circled, probably over some roadkill. He smiled when he saw them. In Tibet, they had something called sky burials. People would actually cut their loved ones into pieces and set those pieces at the top of a hill for the birds to eat. In that way, they believe, their spirits would be released into the heavens.

He wasn't sure if Beulah's death would absolve her of her sins so she too could go to heaven, but that wasn't his choice. That was up to God. It was his job to make sure that wherever she went, she didn't go there easily.

CHAPTER TWENTY ONE

"So the husband's clean?"

"As a whistle," Faith told Missy over the phone. "He's respecting Mandy's memory by refusing to seek vengeance for her death."

"Well, I guess I oughta take my hat off to him for that," she said, "instead of being pissed off that we're back to square one again."

"I'm right there with you," Faith said. "It's really frustrating."

"I don't suppose you have any other nuggets for us?" Michael asked.

"No," Missy said, downcast. "Sorry."

Michael sighed. "That's all right. We'll keep looking."

He hung up and groused, "Another day in the life."

Faith felt something nagging at the back of her mind. The killer was careful to bury his victims near members of their own families. That was a connection between the three victims, one they hadn't focused on before.

Why bury them with family? What was the motivation?

The killer valued family. He wanted family to be together.

Amanda Harrison's family wasn't together anymore. Not until they too died and were buried near her.

The nagging in the back of Faith's mind grew to an almost audible buzz. She called Missy back and said, "Missy, does Amanda Harrison have any other living relatives in the Houston area?"

"Other relatives? I'm not sure, let me look it up and call you back."

She hung up and Faith exchanged a look with Michael.

"You think the family is the key?" Michael asked.

"I think so," Faith said. "It's one thing that ties all three victims together, one thing that we haven't looked at before now."

"Fingers crossed," Michael said.

Turk barked agreement.

Faith's phone buzzed. She answered immediately and turned the speaker on.

"Mandy had a brother," Missy said, "Carter Barkley. He's forty-five years old now, he was thirty-five when she died. He was on scene when she was hit. Looks like he was on his way to surprise her with a visit when he saw the accident. Followed her to the hospital and stayed with her until she went home."

"Perfect," Faith said.

"That's not even the best part," Missy said. "Get this. Carter was a history professor at the University of Texas in Austin, but he quit after Mandy died. Guess what job he took?"

"What?"

"Night watchman at a cemetery. Specifically the Herbert Walker Memorial Lawn. He's worked there the past ten years."

"Beautiful," Michael said. "What's his home address?"

Missy gave them the address and Faith punched it into the GPS. "Okay, we can be there in fifteen minutes," Faith said.

"We can be there in ten," Missy said, "you want us to wait for you?"

"Hell no. If you see him, keep him there until we can get there to talk to him, but don't wait for us before you stop him."

"You got it, baby doll."

Faith tried not to allow herself to get her hopes up, but she couldn't help it. This one felt different from the others. Maybe it was because for the first time they had a connection to the victims *and* the MO. Maybe it was just a hunch. Either way, she felt that somehow this one was more real than the others, more likely to be their guy.

They rushed to the home, and Faith took deep breaths to stay calm. It wouldn't do for her to get overexcited and lose her composure. She glanced over at Michael to see the same practiced calm on his face. In between them, Turk's head was lifted and alert, and his tail switched back and forth again. She wondered when he had picked up that habit. Maybe he had always had it, and she just recently noticed.

She reached down and scratched him in between his ears. "Almost done, boy."

She knew it was too soon to say that, but this one really did feel different. God, she wanted this to be over.

They reached the address in fifteen minutes, as promised, but when they arrived, Missy met them outside the house with a grim expression.

"He's not home. I called his job, and they said he doesn't start until midnight."

The graveyard shift. The irony wasn't lost on Faith.

"Okay," she said, nodding. "That's fine. Let's clear the area and have a few unmarked cars stake the house out. Michael and I will split up and take some officers to search cemeteries in the area. Better yet, let's put out an APB and get the whole department on it. He's probably staking out his next scene. We'll put his description out there, and hopefully someone will…"

Her voice trailed off when she saw a beat-up white van turn down the street, then stop when it saw the police cars. She caught a brief glimpse of the driver and saw the expression of shock on his face. Then his eyes narrowed.

"That's him!" Faith called. "Stop that van!"

She, Michael, and Turk sprinted toward their own car as the driver of the white van spun the wheel. The van skidded as he turned around, but before he could accelerate away from his pursuers, two police cruisers came barreling around the other corner and slammed into the van from the front. He started to reverse, and Faith and Michael dove to the side to avoid the crash.

Faith looked up to see Missy standing with her gun drawn, an old blue steel revolver that looked exactly like what a detective in Texas should carry. She took careful aim at the van's tires and cracked off six shots. Faith heard the pops where they impacted, but the van continued to reverse. Carter backed up until he reached the next street corner, then tried to spin around and head toward the main road. When he spun, his damaged tires finally blew. The van careened to one side, hovered lazily in the air for a moment, then came back down on its wheels.

The driver's door flew open and a huge man climbed out of the van and began to sprint away with explosive speed.

Not as explosive as Turk. The big dog rushed after him, barking and growling. Carter turned toward the German shepherd, then stopped and squared his stance, preparing to fight Turk. A crazed grin spread across his face and he lifted his fists.

An image flashed through Faith's mind of Trammell, wearing his own grin, raising a spade over his head moments before splitting Turk's skull with it. She drew her handgun and shouted, "Stand down or I'll fucking kill you!"

The suspect looked up at Faith, eyes widened in shock at the vehemence of the command. After a moment, he straightened and raised his hands over his head. "I surrender!" he called.

Turk leapt into the air and planted all four feet squarely on his chest, throwing him to the ground. Carter landed with a grunt and kept his hands extended over his head, grinning in spite of Turk's snarling face inches from his own.

Faith arrived a moment later and got her first good look at the man she was now sure was their killer. He was in phenomenal shape. He looked like a powerlifter, with massive shoulders and tree trunks for legs. More tellingly, he was covered in dirt.

He grinned at her and said cheekily, "Good evening, ma'am. Can I help you with something?"

"Where is the victim?" Faith asked immediately.

He lifted one hand and waggled a finger to correct her. "Target."

One of the officers caught up and turned Carter over, pulling first one hand behind his back, then the other, handcuffing him. Carter didn't resist, which was probably a good thing. It would take a half-dozen Tasers to put him down. Looking at him, she wasn't surprised at all that he could dig a grave and bury a body in a coffin singlehandedly and then fill the grave all in a single night. He probably didn't even break a sweat doing it.

"Keep him here," Faith said, "I want to talk to him."

The officer obliged, lifting Carter to a sitting position.

"Where is the *victim*?" Faith repeated, emphasizing the word.

He chuckled. "No, you already broke the rules with the last three targets. The last target you would have rescued if I hadn't gotten lucky with that open grave."

Well, there's one question answered, Faith thought.

"But that's not the game," he said. "They don't get professional help. They have to rely on the mercy of God and the compassion of their fellow citizens. My target has the only chance she'll get."

Faith glanced over at the van. Missy turned to her and shook her head, indicating the van was empty. Turk took a menacing step closer to Carter and growled, but Carter only grinned down at the dog. Faith's eyes narrowed. "Things will be much easier for you if you tell me where I can find her."

He met Faith's eyes, and though he still grinned, his eyes and his words were deadly serious and completely devoid of humor. "There's no help for me, Special Agent. My sister's dead."

Faith looked at Michael, and the same frustration showed on his face.

The same determination showed as well.

She turned back to Carter but addressed Missy. "Detective St. George, do me a favor and pull up the file on Amanda Harrison. I need to know everyone involved in her medical care starting from the paramedics who picked her up."

Carter laughed. "Good luck getting through all of those names before she dies."

Faith smiled thinly. "Well, at least we know it's a she."

Carter's smile faded, and Faith felt a rush of satisfaction. "Have a seat for me, Mr. Carter," she said. "This won't take long."

***

An hour later, Faith didn't feel the same. Night was approaching fast, and depending on where Carter had buried the body, they only had a few hours left to find it. Missy was calling different cemeteries asking them to check for freshly dug unauthorized graves while she and Michael worked through the list.

Even with the males eliminated, it was a long list. There were over a dozen different nurses and several doctors besides Ames who cared for Mandy, not to mention the orderlies, specialists, and hospital security. They had a team of officers working through portions of the list with them, contacting the list members and in some cases their workplaces or family members to ensure they were safe and accounted for.

One by one, they checked names off. The list dwindled, which meant they were getting closer, at least Faith hoped. Part of her worried that the final target could be someone not directly related to her care. She wondered if she should call Ariel, Hucksley's assistant, just to make sure she was safe.

Then Michael called for her attention. She walked over to see him on the phone. "Okay, Mr. Ford. We'll find her. If she comes home, or you hear from her, call us immediately."

He hung up and looked at Faith. "Beulah Ford. She was the discharge nurse who released Amanda Harrison."

Faith privately marveled that Carter would choose the discharge nurse as his final victim when she was probably less involved with her care than anyone else in the hospital, but then again, murderers rarely made sense.

She looked over at him and said loudly, "Beulah Ford?"

Fear flashed across Carter's face, briefly but long enough that Faith caught it. "Yeah, that's her," she said to Michael.

"We need to figure out where her family was buried," Michael said. "Fast. She's been in the ground for at least an hour, maybe more than that."

Faith called Missy over. She said something into her cell phone, then hung up and jogged over to Faith. "What is it?"

"We need to know where the relatives of a Mrs. Beulah Ford, maiden name Cartwright, are buried."

"That's the victim?"

"That's her. She was the discharge nurse at the hospital where Mandy was treated."

"You'll never find her!" Carter called. "I didn't leave a bell this time!"

"Get him out of here!" Faith called to the officers watching him.

Carter laughed and said, "I'll see you soon, Special Agent!"

Oh yes, you will, she thought.

Missy made a call. After a moment, she shouted, "Well, tell him to get his ass back now and he can finish his sandwich later, we have a dying victim in peril!" A few moments later, she said, "Yeah, I need to know where some people are buried. Can you look through the obits and tell me where they're buried?"

There was a brief pause, then she sighed with relief. "Okay, thank you."

She hung up and turned to Faith. "Greenhouse Memorial Lawn. It's about five minutes from here. We have a fresh grave too. It's got a headstone, but we know that he takes opportunities."

"Let's go there," Faith said.

Missy spoke briefly with the officers in charge of transporting Carter Barkley back to the station, then headed to her own vehicle. Michael and Faith jogged back to their own vehicle, where Turk already waited, pacing impatiently.

The vehicle containing Carter started toward the jail, accompanied by another cruiser. The two other vehicles flanked the three federal agents as they headed toward Greenhouse Memorial Lawn.

Faith obviously couldn't see Carter Barkley in the back of a cruiser that was now a quarter-mile away and counting. If she had, she would have seen him smile.

CHAPTER TWENTY TWO

Faith kicked at the nearest headstone, hard enough that she felt her hips ring from the force of the blow. "Dammit!" she shouted.

Turk licked Faith's hand softly, trying to calm her down. It kept her from risking a broken foot again but didn't drive away the frustration she felt.

"Let's keep looking," Michael said. "Maybe he didn't bury her in a plot this time."

Faith nodded, running her fingers back through her hair. Michael immediately started directing the officers and the diggers the cemetery had lent them. They fanned out and started looking through the grounds, looking for any sign of freshly dug earth. The fresh grave they had been alerted to was a bust.

"We could be in the wrong cemetery," Missy said. "He could be misdirecting us."

Faith recalled the flash of fear on Carter's face and shook her head. "No, Beulah Ford is our victim." She thought for a moment. "But we could be in the wrong cemetery." She looked at Missy. "Whatever number you called, call them back. Tell them we need more names. Anyone related to Beulah Ford buried in the area. Tell them to go back decades, a century if they have to. We need to cast a wider net."

She looked at the sky, which had darkened to night, then back down at her phone. Her heart sank. It was nearing an hour since they left Carter's house, two hours since they discovered Beulah was their victim.

Who knew how long she had been buried before they caught Carter.

Missy dialed the number and Faith paced around the nearest gravestone to ease her tension. Turk trotted next to her for support, and she reached down and absently stroked his fur. "Can you smell her, boy?" she asked.

Turk looked up at her, and his plaintive stare told her he was as anxious as she was. She patted his cheek and forced a smile. "It'll be okay, boy. We'll get her out. We've made plenty of last-minute rescues."

This time, though, the ticking clock was ticking a lot faster, and they didn't know where to go.

"Shit!" Missy cried.

Faith snapped her head to the detective, who said, "Okay, thank you," into her phone, then looked up at Faith. For the first time since meeting her, Faith could see real fear in her eyes.

"Beulah's maternal grandparents are buried in the churchyard of the Church of Galilee."

"Wonderful," Faith said. "Where's the Church of Galilee?"

"It doesn't exist anymore," Missy said, "but when it did exist, it was in Edna."

"Where's Edna?"

"About an hour and a half west of here."

Faith's heart, which had lifted slightly when Missy told her of the new location, sank once more to her feet. She kept her cool, however. She had no choice.

"All right," she said, "let's get going."

Missy nodded and called on the radio for everyone to get to their vehicles. Five minutes later, they were accelerating at breakneck speed toward Edna, sirens flashing, loudspeaker announcing to other cars to get out of their way.

An hour and a half to Edna. At the pace they were driving, they could make that in an hour. That meant at least four and a half hours since Beulah was buried, but more likely over five.

They were too late. There was a shot, but it was a very thin shot. Even if they found the grave right away, it would be at least an hour after they arrived before they got her out. Beulah would have to get very lucky, and so would her aspiring rescuers.

Hold on, Beulah, she thought. *Just hold on*.

***

The Church of Galilee had been closed for over thirty years according to Missy, but it looked as though it had been closed for over a century. The building itself was half collapsed and overgrown with ivy and weeds. The cemetery was completely covered in more weeds, and the headstones were faded and covered in lichen and mold. It looked exactly like a place where someone would be buried alive.

The news only got worse when they jumped out of the car. There were no fewer than four freshly dug graves, spaced out across the cemetery. Missy started the officers digging but the thin chance they had was now no chance at all.

Faith looked at Michael, and Michael said, "I called for someone to bring some diggers, but the nearest help is an hour away. They're putting a rush on it, but…"

He didn't finish the thought. He didn't have to.

Faith thought of Carter's haughty grin and her blood began to boil. "That bastard," she spat. "That fucking bastard."

"I know," Michael said, "but don't give up yet. Maybe we'll get lucky."

Faith thought for a moment and said, "Tell everyone to work on one grave at a time. If we dig all four at once, we have no chance. We won't get to the bottom of any of them fast enough to save her. If we're going to get lucky, then it *will* have to be luck."

Michael nodded. "Turk hasn't smelled anything?"

Faith looked at Turk, who was pacing through the cemetery, nose to the ground. "Not yet."

He nodded again. "Well, keep him looking. He found the suit jacket earlier, maybe he'll find Beulah."

Or maybe he'll find her scrubs and another gloating note, she thought but didn't say aloud.

She called to Turk to keep looking and joined the others in starting on the first grave. They worked for about ten minutes before Turk started barking excitedly. Faith turned to see him pawing at the ground a few dozen yards away.

She walked closer and frowned. The area where Turk was digging didn't appear fresh. The dirt over the top was gray and hard-packed and dotted with weeds. She shared a look with Michael, who lifted his hands. *Your call.*

She looked back at Turk, who barked anxiously at her and looked down at the small hole he had created with his front paws. Faith hesitated a moment longer, then decided to trust her dog. She called for everyone to dig where Turk had called them. A few of the officers exchanged glances, but when Missy immediately jogged over to the new location and drove her spade into the earth, they headed over.

After a few minutes, it was clear that underneath the top layer of carefully placed old earth was freshly dug dirt. Faith felt a leap of joy. They were on the right track.

They dug for about twenty minutes before they hit something. "Keep going!" Faith cried. "Double time!"

They increased their pace. Faith felt a stitch burning in her side, but she pushed through the pain, tossing spadeful after spadeful of dirt out of the way. They saw a hint of something brown and kept going.

Then Faith saw the antlers. The killer had buried a deer. It was another decoy.

"God*dammit!"* she swore, tossing her shovel to the ground. She sat down and dropped her face into her hands.

"Don't give up," Missy insisted. "We'll go back to the other grave."

She immediately directed her officers to do just that, but Faith could see the despair in her eyes as well. Michael shared a look with Faith, and the exhaustion in his eyes and the slump in his shoulders told her he had given up as well.

"That asshole," she whispered. "That asshole."

Turk, still digging feverishly around the deer, looked up. When he saw that the others had left, he barked sharply three times. Everyone turned to look at him. He barked insistently, dug for a few more seconds around the deer, then looked up plaintively at them and barked again.

When they hesitated, he growled irritably and began digging around the deer again.

No, not around the deer. *Under* the deer.

Faith's eyes widened. "It's under the deer!" she called. "Beulah's under the deer!"

The police officers looked at each other, clearly not sure whether to believe her or not.

"Move your asses!" Missy barked. "Now!"

They jumped as though they had been tased and rushed back toward the grave. One officer helped Michael lift the deer carcass out of the grave, then they began to dig again. Turk grew more excited as they continued to dig, barking encouragement and running in circles around them.

They dug for another twenty minutes before Faith's shovel once more hit something solid. "Got it!" she cried.

The others quickly dug around the dirt, revealing a plain wooden coffin, the same design as the one in which they found William Hucksley.

Faith leapt into the grave and pulled at the lid. It was nailed shut.

"Shovel!" she called.

Michael tossed one down to her, then jumped in after her with his own shovel. Missy radioed for an ambulance ASAP while Michael and

Faith jammed their shovels under the lid and struggled to pry it open. Turk looked over the lip of the grave and whined plaintively.

Finally, the lid gave. It opened with a soft hiss as the air pressure equalized. She threw the lid open to reveal the pale, still body of Beulah Ford.

Her lips were blue and there were purple circles under her eyes. Her fingers were bloody from where she had struggled to open the grave.

Her eyes were closed, and when Faith felt for a pulse, it was still.

No! It was there! She still had a pulse! It was weak and irregular, but it was there.

Faith immediately dropped to her knees. "She's still alive!" she called. Then she stooped over and began CPR. She breathed in deeply, then covered Beulah's nose, opened her mouth, and exhaled. She repeated the action three times, then began chest compressions.

"Come on, Beulah," Faith whispered. "Come on."

"How long until the ambulance gets here?" Michael called.

"Two minutes!" Missy shouted down.

"Come on, Beulah," Faith said. "We're right here. Don't go away. Stay with us."

She continued CPR until the ambulance sirens sounded in the distance.

"Come on, Beulah," she said again. "You'll be okay. Help is here."

Beulah's eyes flew open. She gasped, then coughed hard. She gasped again and grabbed Faith's arm, eyes staring wildly.

"It's okay," Faith said. "You're safe."

She coughed again, then gasped, then started breathing steadily. "Oh my God," she said, her voice thin and hoarse.

Faith laughed, overcome with relief. "You're okay," she said. "We got you."

Beulah grabbed Faith's arm again and looked into her eyes. "Are you an angel?" she asked.

Faith grinned. "Well, that's not the word most people use, but I'll take it."

Above her, Turk barked excitedly, leaping and licking random hands and faces in celebration. Faith looked up at the sky where the Big Dipper hung lazily from the invisible line that connected it to the North Star.

It was a beautiful night.

CHAPTER TWENTY THREE

Michael, Faith, and Turk walked into the interrogation room where Carter Barkley sat. He was chained to the floor with thick iron shackles, his hands similarly shackled to a stainless steel table that, like the steel chair he sat on, was welded to the floor.

He looked up and smiled at the two agents when they walked in. Turk growled low in his throat, and his grin widened. “Hi there, buddy,” he said. “I’d rub your belly for you, but they got me all tied up.”

Turk bared his teeth in a snarl, a threat that Carter seemed to find funny. He chuckled, then looked up at the two agents. “Did you find her yet?”

“We found her,” Michael said. “She’s being treated at Houston Regional as we speak.”

Carter froze, staring blankly up at him. “She’s alive?” he asked tonelessly.

Michael couldn’t resist a gloating smile. “Yep,” he said, “she’s going to be fine.”

“No,” Carter said, equally tonelessly. Then his face screwed up into a look of rage. “No, no, no, no, *no!*” he cried, his voice gradually rising until it was a shout. He jerked against his bonds, powerful muscles bulging. One shirt sleeve actually tore, and Michael could see the thickly veined bicep underneath.

Carter turned hateful eyes to Michael and Faith and shouted, “You assholes! You jerks! You…”

He finished the sentence with a wordless roar and strained at his bonds again. Michael wasn’t particularly proud of the glee he felt watching the big killer reduced to a completely impotent prisoner due to his bonds, but he wasn’t particularly upset about it either.

Carter struggled for a few more seconds, then gave up and stilled, shaking with fury. “You assholes,” he whispered. “You ruined everything.”

“Gee,” Michael said sarcastically. “I’m awful sorry we didn’t let you get away with murdering someone else.”

“She was a murderer, you dick-breath fuck!” Carter shouted. “She was…” He pressed his lips firmly together and took several deep breaths to calm himself.

When he spoke again, his tone was calm. “You know, in many ancient cultures, such as the ancient Israelites, when someone was murdered, the people responsible were delivered to the victim’s next of kin. The next of kin could choose to release the murderers or have them killed. He could even kill them himself if he so chose.”

“That so?” Michael said. “Hmm. Too bad that’s not how it works here. I won’t lie though. I would love to see William Hucksley’s son drive a knife through your heart.”

Faith shot Michael a warning glance and turned back to Carter. “Why?” she asked. “Why did you kill them? Hucksley, I understand—not that I condone it, but I understand. The others, though. Marvin Prescott has a five-year-old daughter. She’ll never see her daddy again.”

“And I’m sorry for her,” Carter said, “but a lot of murderers have children. We don’t spare their lives. Would you spare me from judgment if I had a child?”

“How the hell did Marvin kill your sister?” Michael said. “Come on, Carter. How can you believe that?”

“He didn’t move fast enough,” Carter said. “He was laughing and joking with his buddies like she was a damned dog and not a human being.” He looked at Turk and added, “No offense.”

He lifted his eyes to Michael and said, “Amanda was the most beautiful person this world has ever had the pleasure of knowing. She was sweet and kind and wonderful. And that…” His lip trembled, and he didn’t finish whatever insult came to his mind. “He fucking treated her like she was… just some animal. And the doctors. I mean, we got there, and they had her *wait*! She was bleeding to death, and they made her wait while they brought in some idiot kid who had laid his bike down on the freeway. Dr. Ames made her wait. What… I just don’t get it.”

“She treated Amanda like any other patient,” Faith said. “She must have felt that the other patient’s condition was more urgent.”

“Fuck that other kid!” Carter shouted. “What? Some dumbass who can’t ride a motorcycle is supposed to be as important as my sister? My beautiful sister who brought joy to everyone she met?”

Michael decided not to mention that his beautiful sister was dancing in the middle of the road, probably drunk, when she got hit. He didn’t want to drag Amanda's memory through the mud because of her brother's psychosis.

He did say, "So you killed them because you thought your sister should have been treated like she was better than everyone else?"

"She *was* better than everyone else!" Carter replied, frowning at Michael, lower lip jutted in a pout. "She was *so* much better than they were. She *did* deserve to be treated first."

Michael shared a look with Faith. She shook her head, and he got the unspoken message. They wouldn't get anywhere with this guy. Michael had one more thing to say before they left, though.

"Have you kept in touch with Fred?"

"Her husband? No, I haven't. Not in years. He's a good guy. I like him, I just… being around him reminded me too much of Mandy. I couldn't be around him anymore."

Michael nodded. He paused a moment, then said, "If you had, he might have told you that Mandy wouldn't have wanted you to take revenge on her behalf."

"He would have been right too," Carter admitted easily. "She would have told me to leave the targets alone and move on. To try to be happy." He smiled wistfully. "She always saw the best in people. She always wanted everyone to be happy." He looked back up at Michael and his smile faded. "I killed these people for myself. I'm not as strong as Mandy. I wanted them to suffer, so I made them suffer."

"So you never intended for them to escape," Faith said.

He hesitated a moment, but then said, "No. No, I guess not. I left them a chance because it was more than they left Mandy, but I didn't want them to take it. I wanted them to suffer." He smiled again, the triumphant smile he wore when they entered. "And they did. Almost all of them." He met Michael's eyes and said, "Three out of four ain't bad, right?"

Michael didn't answer. He stood and motioned for Faith to follow him out. Turk growled one last time at Carter, then turned and followed the two agents.

Faith drove them to the bar where they would meet Missy for drinks to celebrate the successful conclusion of their case. Michael wasn't in a celebratory mood. All he could picture in his mind was Faith sitting in the chair in the abandoned barn where Jethro Trammell had kept her. He recalled the dozens of cuts that crisscrossed her body, the odd bulges where severed tendons had caused her muscles to bunch grotesquely.

He had never told Faith—or anyone—that he had done this, but when he looked at her and saw her reduced to that state, he had nearly drawn his service weapon and emptied the entire clip into Trammell's lifeless head.

He didn't condone Carter Barkley's actions. Not at all.

But he could understand them.

***

Michael half-expected the house to be empty when he arrived. So when he opened the door and Ellie flew into his arms and pressed her lips to his, it was a half-second before he overcame his surprise and kissed her back. Her arms snaked behind his head and tangled in his hair, and when he lifted her off the ground, she wrapped her legs tightly around his waist.

Twenty minutes later, she lay with her head on his chest, smiling softly and sliding her finger softly up and down his navel. "I missed you," she said.

It was the first words either of them had spoken. "I missed you too," he replied, stroking her hair. "I'm sorry we fought before I left. I didn't stay in the same room as Faith this time. I got my own—"

She pushed herself up and kissed him softly, interrupting him. "Shh," she said when she pulled away. "You don't need to apologize."

"Still," he said, "I don't like that we left it like that."

"Me either," she said, "but we're adults. We both know that sometimes we're going to fight."

"I know, but—"

"But—" she continued, lifting her hand to silence him, "we know that we love each other, no matter what." Her smile widened. "And," she added, "soon, we'll be able to memorialize that love."

He stared at her, eyes widening. "You mean…"

She nodded. "This morning. My attorney just faxed the papers."

A wide grin spread across Michael's face. He pulled the laughing Ellie into his arms and kissed her deeply. When he pulled away, she gasped, cheeks flushed, and said, "My God, Michael! You have to let me breathe or you won't get a chance to marry me."

"So marry me tonight," he said. "We'll go right now."

She giggled. "Well, it will be two to four weeks before the divorce is recorded in the state's records, but once that happens, we'll head straight to the nearest courthouse and I'll make you mine. Sound good?"

He rolled on top of her, fast enough that she gasped again.

"*You* sound good," he growled.

She gasped once more before his lips met hers. She wrapped her arms around him, and they were one again.

CHAPTER TWENTY FOUR

David locked the door to the office, checked it, then turned and headed to his car. Faith watched, smirking, as he fiddled with his keys, not realizing she was there until he was only a few feet away.

He gasped and jumped when he saw her, and she laughed. "You really need to be more aware of your surroundings," she said. "Someone could be following you, and they wouldn't even have to try to hide themselves."

"Well, how are they going to get to me when the baddest girl on the planet is stalking me too? They'll never make it past you."

"Damn straight," she said. "You're mine, whether you like it or not."

He chuckled. "So you're going to keep following me until I agree to take you back?"

"I might even kidnap you," she said.

"Sounds dangerous," he said, smiling.

"Don't funk with my heart," she replied, straight-faced.

David's brow furrowed. "What?"

"It's an old song," Faith replied, blushing. "Never mind. Just pretend I said something clever."

David shook his head. "Oh, Faith," he said with an exasperated sigh. "You know, I realized something when you last accosted me at my place of business."

"What's that?" she asked.

"I really missed you," he said. "The best day I've had in the past three months is the day you dragged me out for coffee and told me you wanted me back."

"Even though I won't let go of the Copycat Killer case?"

He took a deep breath, and Faith feared she had ruined the moment, but he surprised her by saying, "Yes, even though you won't let it go." Seeing Faith's surprise, he explained, "If one of my patients needed an emergency visit, I would drop everything to go do what I could. Even if I had to leave you at the altar and reschedule our wedding, I would do my job. And that's just to save one animal's life."

He shook his head. “The Copycat Killer has killed thirty people now. He needs to be put down.” He met Faith’s eyes. “I can’t be upset with you just because you’re the best person to do that. I don’t love that you have to be the one to chase the bad guys, but I’m glad you’re on our side.”

She smiled and lifted a hand to caress his cheek. “Can I kiss—”

Before she could even finish the question, he pulled her close and kissed her deeply. She wrapped her arms around him and sighed, melting into his embrace.

She had made a life out of being strong. It felt so good to let someone else be strong, even if it was only for a moment.

EPILOGUE

Faith walked up the stairs to Clark's apartment, her heart pounding uneasily. No one had heard from him in two days. He had sent a cryptic text to the Boss saying he was taking time off due to a family emergency but hadn't answered the Boss's request to know when he was coming back.

The Boss had texted him every day since but hadn't received a response. Faith's own messages had gone unanswered. The Boss wanted to wait one more day before calling the police for a wellness check, but Faith had a bad feeling that she couldn't shake.

She knew that Gordon had a hidden past that even the Boss didn't know about. If that past had come back to haunt him, then he could be in danger. She needed to know that he was okay. She wasn't sure if she would find Gordon here, but if he *had* gone off half-cocked to take care of some loose thread from his past, she might find the clues she needed here.

She rang the doorbell and waited. There was no answer.

Next to her, Turk whined. She reached down and patted the big dog's head.

Turk's fear did little to help her own anxiety. She took a deep breath and let it out slowly, then knocked on the door.

There was no answer.

It was still light outside, and Faith was suddenly grateful that she had decided to drop by during the day rather than at night. That was a completely irrational feeling. She knew as well as anyone that disaster could befall during the day just as much as it could at night, but her instinctive primate brain grasped at the comfort that came from knowing the sun still shone.

She knocked again, and when there was still no answer, she took another deep breath and pulled the bobby pin and the jeweler's screwdriver from her pocket. She looked around to make sure that no one was watching. The last thing she needed was to have to explain herself to the police.

No one was watching, so she bent over and worked the pin and the screwdriver into the lock. After a few minutes, she felt the lock click open and turned the handle.

The smell assaulted Turk a half-second before it hit her, and he jerked back. Faith's hand went instinctively to her shoulder holster.

Then the smell hit her. She gasped and staggered back as the coppery-sweet scent of blood flooded her senses. She had spent nearly all of her adult life around blood, but this wasn't just anyone's blood. This was her friend's blood, her mentor's blood.

She held out a thin hope that she was wrong, but when she walked inside and saw the body lying in front of the coat closet, her hope disappeared. She closed the door and forced down her nausea as she walked over to the prone body of Supervisory Special Agent Gordon Clark. A nine-iron lay under his limp left hand.

He had tried to defend himself against whoever had killed him.

"Oh Gordon," she said softly. "Oh God. I'm so sorry."

She knelt down and softly stroked his thinning hair. "I'm so sorry," she repeated.

Next to her, Turk whined. He too, was uncharacteristically affected by this scene. Perhaps he felt guilty for his initial dislike of Gordon and regretted that he couldn't make it up to the deceased agent.

Faith allowed herself a moment longer of grief, then stood. In a few minutes, she would call the police and report the death, but before she did that, she wanted to look at the scene herself. A voice in her head told her that she couldn't allow herself to become obsessed over another killer, but Clark was her friend. She wanted to know what happened to him. If it turned out that the mafia had found him and called a hit on him, then she could bring that to the Boss's attention and make it a federal case without needing to go through the red tape that normally entailed. It might mean bringing whoever was responsible to justice faster.

It didn't take much experience to see there had been a struggle. The living room and dining room were torn to pieces. The couch was overturned and the TV was smashed to pieces, along with the stand. The kitchen table and one of the chairs was splintered and debris lay strewn across the laminate floor.

Clark hadn't gone down easy. That brought an odd comfort to Faith. Maybe it was the Marine in her, but she was glad that Clark had made his murderer work for it.

She couldn't see any sign of forced entry. The killer had either been allowed in or, more likely, had broken in the same way Faith had.

She looked around a few more minutes but couldn't find anything that gave a hint of who might have done this. She would have to wait for the cyber unit to crack into his computer before she could check his emails and see if there were any clues there.

She sighed and looked down at Turk. "Well," she said, "let's get the cavalry over here and figure out who hurt our friend."

Turk whined dejectedly and sat, placing his head in between his front paws. Faith stooped and scratched him behind his ear. "I know," she said softly. "Me too, buddy."

She looked up and stopped. When Turk felt her hand still, he looked up at her, then followed her eyes. He got to his feet and Faith stood.

They both crossed to the folded scrap of paper that lay sticking just past the door. Faith bent over and picked up the scrap. It was a piece of paper from a notepad, folded over twice. It was high-quality, soft, and slightly thicker than normal notepaper. A little print of a daisy sat at the bottom.

She unfolded the paper. As she read the note, her eyes widened in shock. Her mouth dried out, and her knees began to tremble slightly, but she noticed none of those physical reactions. Her mind was focused entirely on the message written on the paper.

Sorry to have to take him from you like this, the note read, *but he was getting too Bold.* She noted the capitalization of that word. *You'll be happy to know that he fought like a true warrior, a Prince, if you will.* She gasped and nearly dropped the note when she read that.

The next words nearly caused her knees to buckle. *But, in the end, no veterinary doctor on Earth could save this bull. He died with honor, but he* did *die, and in the end, does it really matter how much honor one has in death?*

The good news, the note continued, *is that you and I can play again, free of distractions. I think you'll agree that the game is better when it is a one-on-one contest of wills: the greatest detective versus the greatest criminal mastermind.*

I wish you luck, Special Agent. You have been by far the best opponent I could ever hope for. I look forward to the conclusion of our struggle.

At the bottom of the paper was a signature. It was written in elegant handwriting, the ink precisely looped and whorled.

He didn't name himself the Copycat Killer. He had escalated.

At the bottom of the paper, in beautiful script, was signed

The Donkey Killer

NOW AVAILABLE!

SO ALONE
(A Faith Bold Mystery—Book 7)

When victims of a new killer are found to have been attacked by dogs, FBI Special Agent Faith Bold knows that her K9 German Shepherd, Turk, will be needed to not only help save the next victim in victim—but also to help her in the fight of her life….

"A masterpiece of thriller and mystery."
—Books and Movie Reviews, Roberto Mattos (re Once Gone)

SO ALONE is Book #7 in a long-anticipated new series by #1 bestseller and USA Today bestselling author Blake Pierce, whose bestseller Once Gone (a free download) has received over 7,000 five star ratings and reviews.

FBI Special Agent Faith Bold doesn't believe she can ever return to the force after the trauma she's been through. Suffering from past demons, she feels unfit for duty and content to retire—until Turk walks into her life.

Turk, a former Marine Corps dog, wounded in battle, suffers from his own demons. But he never lets it show as he gives everything to Faith to get her back on her feet.

Each are slow to warm up to each other, but when they do, they are inseparable. Each is equally determined to hunt down the demons chasing them, whatever the cost, and to watch each other's backs—even at the risk of their own life.

A page-turning and harrowing crime thriller featuring a brilliant and tortured FBI agent, the Faith Bold series is a riveting mystery, packed with non-stop action, suspense, twists and turns, revelations, and driven by a breakneck pace that will keep you flipping pages late into the night. Fans of Rachel Caine, Teresa Driscoll and Robert Dugoni are sure to fall in love.

Future books in the series are now also available.

“An edge of your seat thriller in a new series that keeps you turning pages! ...So many twists, turns and red herrings… I can't wait to see what happens next.”
—Reader review (Her Last Wish)

“A strong, complex story about two FBI agents trying to stop a serial killer. If you want an author to capture your attention and have you guessing, yet trying to put the pieces together, Pierce is your author!”
—Reader review (Her Last Wish)

“A typical Blake Pierce twisting, turning, roller coaster ride suspense thriller. Will have you turning the pages to the last sentence of the last chapter!!!”
—Reader review (City of Prey)

“Right from the start we have an unusual protagonist that I haven't seen done in this genre before. The action is nonstop… A very atmospheric novel that will keep you turning pages well into the wee hours.”
—Reader review (City of Prey)

“Everything that I look for in a book… a great plot, interesting characters, and grabs your interest right away. The book moves along at a breakneck pace and stays that way until the end. Now on go I to book two!”
—Reader review (Girl, Alone)

“Exciting, heart pounding, edge of your seat book… a must read for mystery and suspense readers!”
—Reader review (Girl, Alone)

Blake Pierce

Blake Pierce is the USA Today bestselling author of the RILEY PAGE mystery series, which includes seventeen books. Blake Pierce is also the author of the MACKENZIE WHITE mystery series, comprising fourteen books; of the AVERY BLACK mystery series, comprising six books; of the KERI LOCKE mystery series, comprising five books; of the MAKING OF RILEY PAIGE mystery series, comprising six books; of the KATE WISE mystery series, comprising seven books; of the CHLOE FINE psychological suspense mystery, comprising six books; of the JESSIE HUNT psychological suspense thriller series, comprising thirty-one books; of the AU PAIR psychological suspense thriller series, comprising three books; of the ZOE PRIME mystery series, comprising six books; of the ADELE SHARP mystery series, comprising sixteen books, of the EUROPEAN VOYAGE cozy mystery series, comprising six books; of the LAURA FROST FBI suspense thriller, comprising eleven books; of the ELLA DARK FBI suspense thriller, comprising sixteen books (and counting); of the A YEAR IN EUROPE cozy mystery series, comprising nine books, of the AVA GOLD mystery series, comprising six books; of the RACHEL GIFT mystery series, comprising ten books (and counting); of the VALERIE LAW mystery series, comprising nine books (and counting); of the PAIGE KING mystery series, comprising eight books (and counting); of the MAY MOORE mystery series, comprising eleven books; of the CORA SHIELDS mystery series, comprising eight books (and counting); of the NICKY LYONS mystery series, comprising eight books (and counting), of the CAMI LARK mystery series, comprising eight books (and counting), of the AMBER YOUNG mystery series, comprising five books (and counting), of the DAISY FORTUNE mystery series, comprising five books (and counting), of the FIONA RED mystery series, comprising eight books (and counting), of the FAITH BOLD mystery series, comprising eight books (and counting), of the JULIETTE HART mystery series, comprising five books (and counting), of the MORGAN CROSS mystery series, comprising five books (and counting), and of the new FINN WRIGHT mystery series, comprising five books (and counting).

An avid reader and lifelong fan of the mystery and thriller genres,

Blake loves to hear from you, so please feel free to visit www.blakepierceauthor.com to learn more and stay in touch.

BOOKS BY BLAKE PIERCE

FINN WRIGHT MYSTERY SERIES
WHEN YOU'RE MINE (Book #1)
WHEN YOU'RE SAFE (Book #2)
WHEN YOU'RE CLOSE (Book #3)
WHEN YOU'RE SLEEPING (Book #4)
WHEN YOU'RE SANE (Book #5)

MORGAN CROSS MYSTERY SERIES
FOR YOU (Book #1)
FOR RAGE (Book #2)
FOR LUST (Book #3)
FOR WRATH (Book #4)
FOREVER (Book #5)

JULIETTE HART MYSTERY SERIES
NOTHING TO FEAR (Book #1)
NOTHING THERE (Book #2)
NOTHING WATCHING (Book #3)
NOTHING HIDING (Book #4)
NOTHING LEFT (Book #5)

FAITH BOLD MYSTERY SERIES
SO LONG (Book #1)
SO COLD (Book #2)
SO SCARED (Book #3)
SO NORMAL (Book #4)
SO FAR GONE (Book #5)
SO LOST (Book #6)
SO ALONE (Book #7)
SO FORGOTTEN (Book #8)

FIONA RED MYSTERY SERIES
LET HER GO (Book #1)
LET HER BE (Book #2)
LET HER HOPE (Book #3)

LET HER WISH (Book #4)
LET HER LIVE (Book #5)
LET HER RUN (Book #6)
LET HER HIDE (Book #7)
LET HER BELIEVE (Book #8)

DAISY FORTUNE MYSTERY SERIES
NEED YOU (Book #1)
CLAIM YOU (Book #2)
CRAVE YOU (Book #3)
CHOOSE YOU (Book #4)
CHASE YOU (Book #5)

AMBER YOUNG MYSTERY SERIES
ABSENT PITY (Book #1)
ABSENT REMORSE (Book #2)
ABSENT FEELING (Book #3)
ABSENT MERCY (Book #4)
ABSENT REASON (Book #5)

CAMI LARK MYSTERY SERIES
JUST ME (Book #1)
JUST OUTSIDE (Book #2)
JUST RIGHT (Book #3)
JUST FORGET (Book #4)
JUST ONCE (Book #5)
JUST HIDE (Book #6)
JUST NOW (Book #7)
JUST HOPE (Book #8)

NICKY LYONS MYSTERY SERIES
ALL MINE (Book #1)
ALL HIS (Book #2)
ALL HE SEES (Book #3)
ALL ALONE (Book #4)
ALL FOR ONE (Book #5)
ALL HE TAKES (Book #6)
ALL FOR ME (Book #7)
ALL IN (Book #8)

CORA SHIELDS MYSTERY SERIES
UNDONE (Book #1)
UNWANTED (Book #2)
UNHINGED (Book #3)
UNSAID (Book #4)
UNGLUED (Book #5)
UNSTABLE (Book #6)
UNKNOWN (Book #7)
UNAWARE (Book #8)

MAY MOORE SUSPENSE THRILLER
NEVER RUN (Book #1)
NEVER TELL (Book #2)
NEVER LIVE (Book #3)
NEVER HIDE (Book #4)
NEVER FORGIVE (Book #5)
NEVER AGAIN (Book #6)
NEVER LOOK BACK (Book #7)
NEVER FORGET (Book #8)
NEVER LET GO (Book #9)
NEVER PRETEND (Book #10)
NEVER HESITATE (Book #11)

PAIGE KING MYSTERY SERIES
THE GIRL HE PINED (Book #1)
THE GIRL HE CHOSE (Book #2)
THE GIRL HE TOOK (Book #3)
THE GIRL HE WISHED (Book #4)
THE GIRL HE CROWNED (Book #5)
THE GIRL HE WATCHED (Book #6)
THE GIRL HE WANTED (Book #7)
THE GIRL HE CLAIMED (Book #8)

VALERIE LAW MYSTERY SERIES
NO MERCY (Book #1)
NO PITY (Book #2)
NO FEAR (Book #3)
NO SLEEP (Book #4)
NO QUARTER (Book #5)
NO CHANCE (Book #6)

NO REFUGE (Book #7)
NO GRACE (Book #8)
NO ESCAPE (Book #9)

RACHEL GIFT MYSTERY SERIES
HER LAST WISH (Book #1)
HER LAST CHANCE (Book #2)
HER LAST HOPE (Book #3)
HER LAST FEAR (Book #4)
HER LAST CHOICE (Book #5)
HER LAST BREATH (Book #6)
HER LAST MISTAKE (Book #7)
HER LAST DESIRE (Book #8)
HER LAST REGRET (Book #9)
HER LAST HOUR (Book #10)

AVA GOLD MYSTERY SERIES
CITY OF PREY (Book #1)
CITY OF FEAR (Book #2)
CITY OF BONES (Book #3)
CITY OF GHOSTS (Book #4)
CITY OF DEATH (Book #5)
CITY OF VICE (Book #6)

A YEAR IN EUROPE
A MURDER IN PARIS (Book #1)
DEATH IN FLORENCE (Book #2)
VENGEANCE IN VIENNA (Book #3)
A FATALITY IN SPAIN (Book #4)

ELLA DARK FBI SUSPENSE THRILLER
GIRL, ALONE (Book #1)
GIRL, TAKEN (Book #2)
GIRL, HUNTED (Book #3)
GIRL, SILENCED (Book #4)
GIRL, VANISHED (Book 5)
GIRL ERASED (Book #6)
GIRL, FORSAKEN (Book #7)
GIRL, TRAPPED (Book #8)
GIRL, EXPENDABLE (Book #9)

GIRL, ESCAPED (Book #10)
GIRL, HIS (Book #11)
GIRL, LURED (Book #12)
GIRL, MISSING (Book #13)
GIRL, UNKNOWN (Book #14)
GIRL, DECEIVED (Book #15)
GIRL, FORLORN (Book #16)

LAURA FROST FBI SUSPENSE THRILLER
ALREADY GONE (Book #1)
ALREADY SEEN (Book #2)
ALREADY TRAPPED (Book #3)
ALREADY MISSING (Book #4)
ALREADY DEAD (Book #5)
ALREADY TAKEN (Book #6)
ALREADY CHOSEN (Book #7)
ALREADY LOST (Book #8)
ALREADY HIS (Book #9)
ALREADY LURED (Book #10)
ALREADY COLD (Book #11)

EUROPEAN VOYAGE COZY MYSTERY SERIES
MURDER (AND BAKLAVA) (Book #1)
DEATH (AND APPLE STRUDEL) (Book #2)
CRIME (AND LAGER) (Book #3)
MISFORTUNE (AND GOUDA) (Book #4)
CALAMITY (AND A DANISH) (Book #5)
MAYHEM (AND HERRING) (Book #6)

ADELE SHARP MYSTERY SERIES
LEFT TO DIE (Book #1)
LEFT TO RUN (Book #2)
LEFT TO HIDE (Book #3)
LEFT TO KILL (Book #4)
LEFT TO MURDER (Book #5)
LEFT TO ENVY (Book #6)
LEFT TO LAPSE (Book #7)
LEFT TO VANISH (Book #8)
LEFT TO HUNT (Book #9)
LEFT TO FEAR (Book #10)

LEFT TO PREY (Book #11)
LEFT TO LURE (Book #12)
LEFT TO CRAVE (Book #13)
LEFT TO LOATHE (Book #14)
LEFT TO HARM (Book #15)
LEFT TO RUIN (Book #16)

THE AU PAIR SERIES
ALMOST GONE (Book#1)
ALMOST LOST (Book #2)
ALMOST DEAD (Book #3)

ZOE PRIME MYSTERY SERIES
FACE OF DEATH (Book#1)
FACE OF MURDER (Book #2)
FACE OF FEAR (Book #3)
FACE OF MADNESS (Book #4)
FACE OF FURY (Book #5)
FACE OF DARKNESS (Book #6)

A JESSIE HUNT PSYCHOLOGICAL SUSPENSE SERIES
THE PERFECT WIFE (Book #1)
THE PERFECT BLOCK (Book #2)
THE PERFECT HOUSE (Book #3)
THE PERFECT SMILE (Book #4)
THE PERFECT LIE (Book #5)
THE PERFECT LOOK (Book #6)
THE PERFECT AFFAIR (Book #7)
THE PERFECT ALIBI (Book #8)
THE PERFECT NEIGHBOR (Book #9)
THE PERFECT DISGUISE (Book #10)
THE PERFECT SECRET (Book #11)
THE PERFECT FAÇADE (Book #12)
THE PERFECT IMPRESSION (Book #13)
THE PERFECT DECEIT (Book #14)
THE PERFECT MISTRESS (Book #15)
THE PERFECT IMAGE (Book #16)
THE PERFECT VEIL (Book #17)
THE PERFECT INDISCRETION (Book #18)
THE PERFECT RUMOR (Book #19)

THE PERFECT COUPLE (Book #20)
THE PERFECT MURDER (Book #21)
THE PERFECT HUSBAND (Book #22)
THE PERFECT SCANDAL (Book #23)
THE PERFECT MASK (Book #24)
THE PERFECT RUSE (Book #25)
THE PERFECT VENEER (Book #26)
THE PERFECT PEOPLE (Book #27)
THE PERFECT WITNESS (Book #28)
THE PERFECT APPEARANCE (Book #29)
THE PERFECT TRAP (Book #30)
THE PERFECT EXPRESSION (Book #31)

CHLOE FINE PSYCHOLOGICAL SUSPENSE SERIES
NEXT DOOR (Book #1)
A NEIGHBOR'S LIE (Book #2)
CUL DE SAC (Book #3)
SILENT NEIGHBOR (Book #4)
HOMECOMING (Book #5)
TINTED WINDOWS (Book #6)

KATE WISE MYSTERY SERIES
IF SHE KNEW (Book #1)
IF SHE SAW (Book #2)
IF SHE RAN (Book #3)
IF SHE HID (Book #4)
IF SHE FLED (Book #5)
IF SHE FEARED (Book #6)
IF SHE HEARD (Book #7)

THE MAKING OF RILEY PAIGE SERIES
WATCHING (Book #1)
WAITING (Book #2)
LURING (Book #3)
TAKING (Book #4)
STALKING (Book #5)
KILLING (Book #6)

RILEY PAIGE MYSTERY SERIES
ONCE GONE (Book #1)

ONCE TAKEN (Book #2)
ONCE CRAVED (Book #3)
ONCE LURED (Book #4)
ONCE HUNTED (Book #5)
ONCE PINED (Book #6)
ONCE FORSAKEN (Book #7)
ONCE COLD (Book #8)
ONCE STALKED (Book #9)
ONCE LOST (Book #10)
ONCE BURIED (Book #11)
ONCE BOUND (Book #12)
ONCE TRAPPED (Book #13)
ONCE DORMANT (Book #14)
ONCE SHUNNED (Book #15)
ONCE MISSED (Book #16)
ONCE CHOSEN (Book #17)

MACKENZIE WHITE MYSTERY SERIES
BEFORE HE KILLS (Book #1)
BEFORE HE SEES (Book #2)
BEFORE HE COVETS (Book #3)
BEFORE HE TAKES (Book #4)
BEFORE HE NEEDS (Book #5)
BEFORE HE FEELS (Book #6)
BEFORE HE SINS (Book #7)
BEFORE HE HUNTS (Book #8)
BEFORE HE PREYS (Book #9)
BEFORE HE LONGS (Book #10)
BEFORE HE LAPSES (Book #11)
BEFORE HE ENVIES (Book #12)
BEFORE HE STALKS (Book #13)
BEFORE HE HARMS (Book #14)

AVERY BLACK MYSTERY SERIES
CAUSE TO KILL (Book #1)
CAUSE TO RUN (Book #2)
CAUSE TO HIDE (Book #3)
CAUSE TO FEAR (Book #4)
CAUSE TO SAVE (Book #5)
CAUSE TO DREAD (Book #6)

KERI LOCKE MYSTERY SERIES

A TRACE OF DEATH (Book #1)
A TRACE OF MURDER (Book #2)
A TRACE OF VICE (Book #3)
A TRACE OF CRIME (Book #4)
A TRACE OF HOPE (Book #5)

Made in United States
Troutdale, OR
12/26/2023

16456953R00105